Praise for *The Forgotten Girl*

"*The Forgotten Girl* is a story not soon forgotten. Stella's tale is one of abandonment and hope, of perseverance and joy, sorrow and smiles, not unlike so many immigrants from the turn of the last century whose only dream is America. With deft prose, Heather Chapman invites readers on a touching and poignant journey, which summons they will gladly accept."

—Nancy E. Turner, award-winning author of *These is My Words*

"A lovely and moving book. *The Forgotten Girl* is a splendid example of finding beauty amongst the ashes. Stefania, broken yet brave, reminds us of the strength and fortitude of those upon whose backs our country was built. Readers will be pulled in right to the heart of her story."

—Julie Daines, award-winning author of historical fiction novels

"Rich with emotion, *The Forgotten Girl* is a beautiful story of a resilient and unforgettable girl. Through her difficult and at times heartbreaking journey, we are reminded of the power of words, the strength of friendship, and the importance of hope."

—Ashtyn Newbold, author of *Lies and Letters* and *Mischief and Manors*

"Heather Chapman weaves a fascinating story of a young woman's journey from the harsh life of an orphan in Poland to the tenuous life of an immigrant in Baltimore. *The Forgotten Girl* is a map in perseverance and courage. A stunning tale of multiple cultures struggling to make sense of what freedom means, wrapped in the determination to find purpose in their dreams."

—Carolyn Steele, author of *Soda Springs*

"I love historical fiction based on true stories, and *The Forgotten Girl* by Heather Chapman is no exception. Based on her ancestor's life, readers will be drawn into the volatile era of the early Poland, in which many are fleeing to America in search of a better life. Stella is a heroine who's easy to root for, and the setting of both Poland and early America is vibrant, sobering, and inspirational. *The Forgotten Girl* is an engaging story that takes the reader on a journey back through time and reaffirms the spirit of seeking out a better life and securing freedom."

—Heather B. Moore, *USA Today* bestselling author

"I highly enjoyed the rich depth of detail in *The Forgotten Girl.* Chapman captures the reader and takes them on each step of Stella's journey as though we walked beside her."

—Ranee Clark, author of *Love, Jane*

"Stella leaves Poland, searching for belonging, and on the way, discovers heartache, betrayal, friendship, and most of all her own strength. A beautifully told story of a young girl's journey to America, rich with history and engaging characters. I thoroughly enjoyed it."

—Jennifer Moore, author of *Miss Whitaker Opens Her Heart*

THE FORGOTTEN GIRL

A COURAGEOUS GIRL,
A DIFFICULT JOURNEY,
A GUIDING LIGHT.

THE FORGOTTEN GIRL

A COURAGEOUS GIRL,
A DIFFICULT JOURNEY,
A GUIDING LIGHT.

HEATHER CHAPMAN

AUTHOR OF *THE SECOND SEASON*

SWEETWATER BOOKS

An imprint of Cedar Fort, Inc.
Springville, UT

ISBN 13: 978-1-4621-2064-2

Published by Sweetwater Books, an imprint of Cedar Fort, Inc.
2373 W. 700 S., Springville, UT 84663
Distributed by Cedar Fort, Inc., www.cedarfort.com

LIBRARY OF CONGRESS CATALOGING-IN-PUBLICATION DATA

Names: Chapman, Heather, 1986- author.
Title: The forgotten girl / Heather Chapman.
Description: Springville, Utah : Sweetwater Books, An Imprint of Cedar Fort, Inc., [2018]
Identifiers: LCCN 2017038613 (print) | LCCN 2017042028 (ebook) | ISBN 9781462128167 (epub and Moby) | ISBN 9781462120642 ([perfect] : alk. paper)
Subjects: LCSH: Immigrants--Maryland--Baltimore--Fiction. | Polish people--Maryland--Baltimore--Fiction. | Fells Point (Baltimore, Md.), setting. | Nineteen hundreds (Decade), setting. | LCGFT: Historical fiction. | Novels.
Classification: LCC PS3603.H369 (ebook) | LCC PS3603.H369 F67 2018 (print) | DDC 813/.6--dc23
LC record available at https://lccn.loc.gov/2017038613

Cover design by Katie Payne

Edited and typeset by Jessica Romrell

Printed in the United States of America

10 9 8 7 6 5 4 3 2 1

Printed on acid-free paper

For Mark

Other Books by Heather Chapman

The Second Season

Unexpected Love: A Marriage of Convenience Anthology (coauthor)

One

Durliosy, Poland, 1906

Nie ma dymu bez ognia.
Where there is smoke, there is fire.

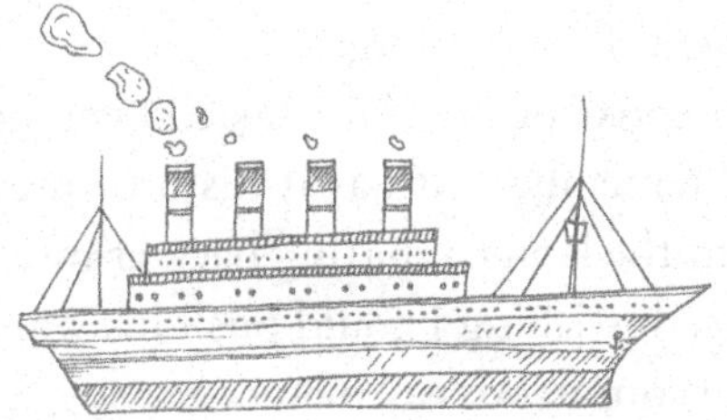

My father used to say that desperation is the death of reason, that once fear seizes the reins, there is no telling where it will take you. Somehow, desperation led me here, standing in front of my brother and his family, begging for something more than this dreary existence.

My mouth is dry, but I try to swallow. "If I were to join Wiktor and Stanislaus in America, you would no longer be burdened with my care. It would be one less mouth to feed, one less worry to carry upon your shoulders."

Jozef shakes his head, and I see his shoulders rise, the hint of hesitation in his stance. His eyes harden, and I think I have lost him.

"Jozef?" I ask, not certain if he hears me.

His jaw juts forward, and the muscle along his bone rises. "You forget," he says, his voice growing deeper. His eyes return to me, the corners of them narrowing into slits. "Poles are not welcome in America."

My hands shake, so I clasp them to my chest, where a kindling has now blistered to a blaze. Hot tears spill from my downcast eyes. *Not welcome?*

"We are not welcome in our own country," I say, rocking back and forth.

Jozef lets out a grunt so deep that it rolls through the room, bouncing along the floorboards and in between the others seated at the table. His hand twists around the back of the chair, and for a moment, I wonder if he means to crush the wood between his fingers.

"At least tell me you have not forgotten your Polish pride." His voice cracks like a whip against a mule.

I shake my head, too angry and stubborn to say anything in reply. I do not forget. I cannot forget.

"When father spoke of the Uprising, did you not hear any of it? Surely, you must remember." It's as if his brown eyes have ignited, the reflection from the lantern spitting back at me.

I shake my head, wishing I could push his words away. But it is too late. His voice commands my memory.

The Uprising against the Russian Empire was the last thing father spoke of before he died. It was the bloodiest battle my father, only a boy then, ever saw. There were too many lives lost, peasants pitted against soldiers. My father spoke of the blood and death, the bodies strewn along the streets. It was a beating down for my people, a reminder that Poland is just a pawn in the game being played by Russia.

And so it was with my father. With no chance of success, thirty-eight years after the Uprising, he led his own revolt. Though his fight was against landholders instead of soldiers, it eventually led to the same outcome—the same loss, the same reminder, the same death by Russian hand.

Jozef does not see, or so he pretends. He pretends he does not see my pain. Maybe he feels it, too. Maybe we share much more than our brown eyes and auburn hair.

Tears flow down my cheek, falling to the ground, much like my misplaced hope. Teeth gritted, I turn to face my brother once more. He has not moved an inch. His hand still clutches the back of the chair. There is a fierceness in his grasp that I fear will turn to me, as it so often does.

"I will hear no more talk of America. Come, sit, you must eat," he says, extending his hand toward me in a beckoning manner. But there is no mistaking; it is a command.

The children are silent, too frightened to touch their meal or make a sound. Even my sister-in-law Mania looks down at her feet.

Too defeated to resist, I pull back my stool, the edge thudding against the leg of the table. It shifts the tabletop, sending the tin plates skidding. Yet it cannot rattle me any more than I already am.

Another grunt, this time Jozef's mouthful muting the thunderous sound.

I sit, staring at my plate. I cannot seem to keep myself from scratching my spoon against the plate, swirling it around the conglomeration of cabbages, onion, mushroom, and an assortment of aging meats. I scoop a spoonful and drop it to my plate, the splattering sound as familiar as the smell. Bigos again. It is all we ever have, if we have anything at all.

The children still do not say a word. My niece's eyes are glistening, a frown stretching across her little lips. She knows nothing of the pain of my parents' deaths, the bleakness of my future. She only hears her father's grunts, feels the mounting tension. It is as thick as molasses. If only it were as sweet.

The whimpering wind against the house is the only noise to counter the scratching of our spoons against the plates. My nephew Casimir's eyes are wide, staring at his now-empty plate. He licks his spoon, searching for missed morsels. But as always, there is nothing left. Nothing more to fill his belly, nothing left to lift my spirits.

Jozef is the last to finish, and he savors each bite, closing his eyes. His jaw moves in a circular pattern, around and around each spoonful.

He exhales and stands, awakening me to his irritation once more. He glances at me, a challenge shining back at me. He nods, pushing his arms into the sleeves of his coat. "I'll feed the animals alone tonight," he says, as if his stare is enough to ward away the designs of my heart.

His exit brings a gust of wind and snow, and it sends a chill down my spine. The clink of the latch sounds, and the room is brighter in an instant. My nephews' uncharacteristic nervousness disappears—little Jozef's shoulders relax, and Casimir sighs in relief. A minute more, and the boys are circling around the table, chasing my niece, Bronia, threatening to tickle her. The pounding of their feet along the floorboards sound and feel like thunder after the stifling silence at dinner.

Bronia giggles, her cheerful exults filling the air. She gasps for breath, her hands hovering above her chest. Her pale face fades to a light blue. Yet it is her wheezing that causes my heart to race.

"I don't want to play," she says, her arms crossing in front of her.

Casimir growls, pulling one of her dark braids. "You always ruin it."

Bronia finds her way to my side, stealing away in the depths of my skirt. She clutches my ankles, her head tucking beneath my chair.

"Hiding in Stella's skirt again, Bronia?" little Jozef asks. He folds his arms, his stringy arms tensing. His lips curve into a smug smirk.

"You cannot hide forever," Casimir whispers.

I cast my darkest glare and swat my hand toward the loft. "Off with you both. Leave your sister alone."

Casimir cowers, and he and little Jozef turn toward the loft.

I stare down at my skirt, stained to a muddy brown and so thin it is almost transparent near the ankles. I lift the edge and look beneath my chair.

Two dark eyes stare up at me. "Ciocia Stella, are they gone?" she asks. Her lashes are curled around wide eyes, and her petal lips quiver. Bronia moves to her knees.

I nod, touching her now pink cheek. I can see my tiny reflection in her glistening eyes, and I smile. She holds so much of my heart.

Bronia's gaze darts toward the loft. "Ciocia Stella, you will keep me safe."

She climbs to my lap and twists the red and brown strands of hair at the nape of my neck, smiling. The small gap between her front teeth is showing, and I cannot help but smile back.

"Stefania," my sister-in-law says, "the table and the dishes. You will have time enough with Bronia." The creases near her brow deepen. "Bronia, you must come to Matka."

Bronia slides away from my skirt toward Mania's outstretched arms. It is always so. Mania cannot stand to see Bronia near me.

The pail of snow hanging above the stove has melted. I dip my rag in it, flinching as my hand hits the ice water. I scrub the plates and spoons with more vigor than usual, the force and chill numbing the tips of my fingers.

Mania reminds me daily of their charity. I deserve much less, she says. I scrub harder, my knuckles beginning to bleed. I am without a place in this world. Sixteen, without a father or a mother.

Mania tosses a fresh pile of mending on the table. Her eyes hover over mine. She spits to the side. "When you are finished," she says, pointing toward the sloppy mound.

I nod, silently cursing. Socks, skirts, trousers, blouses. Each one I have mended already, and each one has new holes. There won't be anything left to mend on Casimir's trousers if he does not take more care.

I pull the chair by the stove, hopeful that the dying embers will warm me. Mania towers over me, her back slumped. She watches each stitch I make. I can sense her anticipation.

A forceful blow sends the door pounding against its frame, and a whistle screeches through the cracks. Mania startles, and I flinch, pricking my finger. Blood drips over the sock.

Without hesitation, Mania sends her own blow across my cheek. It stings, and I instinctively place my other hand over it.

"You sew like a drunken man," she says in her angry Croatian. "You have bloodied the sock. Give it to me, stupid girl." She rips it from my hand and the needle scratches against my arm. "You will never make a good wife," she mumbles, each word full of spite. She points to the loft. "The children. I will sew the socks myself."

I leave without a word, sucking on the end of my finger to stop the blood.

The ladder rattles against the loft with each rung I climb. I am too old and heavy for it, but there is no other place for me to lie my head, no other way to escape my brother and Mania, nowhere else for me to go.

When I reach the top, the boys are wrestling. Jozef has pinned Casimir, and Casimir gasps for breath. Little Jozef hits the wood planks beneath his knees three times.

"You cheated!" Casimir says, rolling away. His face is red from the exertion, a familiar look of defeat.

"You always say that," Jozef says, "but I am stronger."

Casimir yells, throwing a weak fist at his brother.

I catch Casimir's lanky arm mid-air. "That is enough. You both act worse than the animals. Casimir, you cannot hit whenever you are angry."

His eyes narrow to slits. "I am a man; I can hit when I like."

I grip his wrist tighter, my nails sinking in his skin. "You are not one yet. And even then, you will have to learn to control your temper."

Jozef seems satisfied with Casimir's rebuke. He wipes his hands together before raking them through his dark hair.

"Climb into bed," I say.

As always, my niece, Bronia, slips into the covers beside me, resting her messy brown head against my shoulder. Then, the stories begin. Some days they are shorter, some longer, but always, there are stories to be told. Casimir and Jozef fall asleep partway through them each night, but Bronia listens to each word, often begging for more. Tonight, I tell her a story I once heard from my father. I can almost hear his deep voice as I recite the last few lines. But the memory fades more quickly than it came.

Bronia's breathing slows, and she is asleep.

Relief washes over me. The night belongs to me. There is no Mania to breathe down my neck. There is no Jozef to silence my questions. And there are no giggles or cries.

It is colder than usual, and I pull the wool blanket close to my face and breath down it, hopeful it will warm my shivering toes.

Perhaps it will also warm my heart.

Mother died when I was only six. My father did not know how to overcome his grief. To cope, he chose Poland and his fellow farmers. After only being a widower for five years, he followed after Matka to the grave, leaving me, my sister, and my four brothers.

Bronia snuggles into my shoulder, bringing me back to the drafty and dirty loft. I cannot remember much of my mother's care. I wonder if she loved me as I love Bronia. I wonder if she held me close and whispered stories in my ear.

Two

Co było, nie wróci.
What was, won't come back.

Six years old, and I watch the flame flicker. The candle sits in a pool of melted wax, the wick, like our eyelids, drooping lower and lower. But each time I start to drift, I shake myself, somehow feeling that this moment will change everything.

"Matka," I say, clutching her shrunken hand with both of mine. "Why are you sleeping?"

Her lashes flutter. Her face is white, her auburn hair matted against the pillow and drenched in sweat. And yet her body is still.

I tighten my grip, shaking it with each word. "Matka, wake up. The day is here; the sun is almost up." My eyes sting. I see that she is leaving me, like a cloud that floats away when I chase it. "Matka!"

My father crouches beside me, his breath a cloud in the dampness. His eyes harden, and he looks more threatening than comforting. But he reaches for me, his hands grasping at my shoulders. "She is dying, Stefania. Your mother is too sick. She cannot stay much longer."

His tears fall onto my head, and he holds me, clutching my head to his chest. I have never seen him cry before.

Then I feel it—my anger and sadness rolled up into one, a feeling new to my young heart. With a violent movement, I pull away, wiping his tears from my head. I move closer to my mother.

She is not dying. She is only sleeping.

I awake to Bronia's coughing. I rub my eyes, wishing it was just a dream and not something of my past.

Bronia is leaning over me, her loose braids dangling in the space between us. Her big brown eyes are watering from her illness, the edges of her lashes crusted over.

"Good morning, Bronia-sweet," I say, stretching my arms.

She smiles and puts her hand on my face, touching each freckle and feature of my cheek. "I cannot play today," she tells me, "because I am so sick."

I smile, running my fingers along her frayed braids. "Yes, we must get you better."

She nods, pulling the covers to her chin. "Will you stay with me?"

"I would rather stay with you, but I must help Jozef today. He needs me to work with the animals."

"No, Ciocia Stella, I mean, will you always stay here with me?" Bronia's voice cracks. She sits up straight, trying to swallow a cough. Eventually it forces its way out, and her body shakes with the convulsion.

I watch her, aware of the emotion climbing my throat. I would always stay for her. But I cannot not stay for myself.

She cranes her head to the side. Our eyes meet, and I see the question once more in her eyes.

"Bronia, I only know that someday you will grow, and you will not need me."

My niece shakes her head, furrowing her brows. "But, Ciocia, you can't leave me. You are my best friend, and if you go, I will be too sad."

Her stubborn expression is more endearing than persuasive. I giggle, reaching toward her head to pat her hair with my fingers. I feel like she is my own. I hold her close, listening to her breathe. It sounds far too laborious than it should for one so small. I cringe, tightening my embrace.

"Will you tell me more stories tonight?"

I nod. "As soon as I return."

"Then go fast, Stella."

My steps down the rickety ladder shake the loft, wood slats bumping up and down. I see the boys stir in their beds. Casimir is still asleep, his mouth open wide, but he wiggles his shoulders back and forth from side to side.

My brother stirs. "Stefania?" His voice is pained.

"Yes, I am just leaving to feed," I whisper back, hoping not to wake Mania.

He emerges from behind the curtain, a tired but urgent look upon his face. He is still pulling his trousers on, but motions for me to come closer.

I step forward.

He holds a clenched fist toward me. "Here, take this."

I open my hand, and he places a few cold coins in it.

"What is this?" I ask, curious as to what he would have me do with it.

"Stefania, I need you to go to market for me."

I blink in confusion. "I thought we were not going to the market for three more days."

"I cannot go at all. My leg is giving me trouble again. You must go for me, today, now. The cart is packed, and you will stay at Amalia's. Buy some medicine for Bronia while you are there. She is getting worse."

I have never traveled to the market without Jozef. Ostroleka is twelve miles away. I do not want to manage it alone, especially with the cart, in the cold. I have not traded without Jozef. What if I cannot find medicine?

I shake my head.

"The items will sell. This," he says closing his hand around my own, "is only to be used should you need it. It is better you leave now. I would not want you to upset the children." He takes a loaf of bread and wraps it in a cloth, handing it to me.

I stare back at him, anxiousness and reluctance rising in my chest.

Jozef sees my hesitant steps. His jaw tightens, and I watch the muscles along his face rise. He folds his arms across his chest, as if he is daring me to refuse.

It is always thus. There are no choices here.

I nod. "I will go."

The door slams behind me, and I hear Mania yell, likely awakening Casimir and little Jozef for good. "Quiet! Can't a woman get a little sleep?"

I turn toward the barn, the coins clinking together in my hand. I stop, trying to find a safe place for them, my hands running over each pocket. Each one is much too worn with too many holes.

"Sister."

I startle, turning back toward the house. Jozef offers his coat. It is much too large. He is only a few inches taller than me, but his shoulders and arms are strong and thick, mine feminine, petite. Yet I cannot refuse it. It is much warmer than my tattered one.

Pushing my arms through the sleeves, I stoop with the weight of the wool and place the coins in an intact pocket.

He holds out his other hand, pushing a pail of water toward me. "Do take care of yourself."

His words of caution startle me. My eyes meet his, and I notice a gleam of some sort behind his black eyes. It would be foolish to suppose his tone affectionate, but I cannot remember a time he has done anything so kind.

"Thank you, Jozef," I say, looking to the ground.

He says nothing, leaving my side as quickly and quietly as he came.

The cart is already packed. It sits in the corner of the barn, covered with a wool blanket to keep away the dirt. I pull back the makeshift cover, revealing the bottles of milk. There are also eggs, so many that they are overflowing the baskets and in likely the same condition as the milk—frozen over. I pick one up and shake it, hearing the familiar sound of slushed egg against the shell, like a shaker the musicians use during the village festivals. But there is nothing magical about the sound this morning.

If only we could eat them . . . but Jozef says we need the money more.

An assortment of our neighbor's crops—potatoes and cabbages mostly—lie between the bottles and baskets. The cart is full, and I add even more weight by fitting the pail of water and my old coat between the baskets and bottles. The cart is heavy, and I struggle as I pull it across the frosted ground. One mile will be hard enough; I do not know how I will make it twelve.

Perhaps it is better that I am leaving now.

Everything is in front of me; the end seems an eternity away. I do not think I can do this. The wind is cold in my face, and my feet are already frozen in my well-used boots.

Yet somehow, the cart begins to roll along the lane, and it keeps to a steady pace. The downward slopes are heaven-sent, as if God Himself has taken the load for a moment. It has been nearly an hour, and I am only just passing the small parish. Two miles down. I rest for a moment, stretching my back and arms. My legs burn.

My brother and I walk to market at least once a month, but sometimes once a week. Jozef has always pulled the cart, except for short durations when I let him rest. The longest I have pulled the cart, on my own and in good weather, was three miles.

I plunge my hands into the pail of water, cupping the cold liquid to my mouth. I gulp it down until it soothes my burning throat. There is so much farther to go, so I make myself stand. Yet just as I take my first step, I stub my toe against a pointed rock—a timely reminder that things can always get worse.

I curse between my teeth, reeling over at my throbbing toe. But almost as soon as the words slip through my lips, I startle, remembering where I stand. The church. I wince in pain once more, but determine to keep my composure.

The rising sound of wagon wheels against the path rouses me from self-pity, and I turn, startled to see a horse and load pull to a stop behind me. A boy with brown hair and gentle eyes jumps off the side of the cart and runs to me. My heart softens in an instant. It is Andrzejek, my best friend.

"Stella, what are you doing?" he asks, his dark brows knitted together. His light eyes search my expression, resting on my eyes. "Are you alright?"

The wind blows a loose strand of hair across my face, and I turn against the wind, tugging at the inside of Jozef's coat pocket. "Jozef needs me to go to market. And so I am."

"Alone?" His question hangs in the wind, drifting closer.

I nod, trying to conserve my energy.

He gasps. "And you are to pull this load by yourself?"

I say nothing, but Andrzejek sees the answer in my trembling arms and my downcast eyes.

"Hmm," he says, scraping his boot against the gravel. "We will see."

He turns toward his cart, calling for his brother Oliwjer. The two brothers speak, their heads bobbing each time they glance my way.

Before I know it, the two are down beside me and pulling my cart to their wagon. Somehow, they manage to lift my load onto the rickety wagon bed. I hear the milk bottles rattle against one another and see a few cabbages roll to the dirt.

I instinctively reach my arm out, touching Andrzejek's arm. "What are you doing?"

They ignore me, securing the hinged back of their wagon.

"Andrze? Oliwjer?" I ask once more, bending to pick up the fallen cabbages.

Oliwjer smirks, his green eyes grayer in the early light. "Can't you see, Stella? We are putting your cart in our own." He shakes his head and laughs, but his jaw is clenched, his lips pursed. "You cannot walk the whole twelve miles with this load. Your brother thinks you are a man." He pauses, looking me over. He smiles, but I see the pity in his face. "But we know better. We will take you five miles, where the road turns. We are already going that way."

For a moment, I feel my heart crumble, a prayer on the tip of my tongue, but then my pride consumes me. "You are not going that way."

They are silent, their eyes locked on one another.

"You think I am not strong enough." My voice cracks, and I feel my eyes water. *I* do not think I am strong enough.

"Stella," Andrzejek says softly, stepping toward me. He grasps my hand, pulling me toward him. "I know you are strong enough, but that does not mean that you have to do it by yourself."

Oliwjer holds his arms out, gesturing for me to climb up the side of the wagon.

I stand there, uncertain of what to do. My stubborn pride urges me to refuse, yet five miles less of walking and pulling the cart? It seems an answer to a prayer, and it is foolish to refuse. I accept his outstretched hand, smiling in gratitude.

I sit beside Andrzejek, and I can't help but rest my head against his shoulder. He has been my best friend since I was five and has stayed by my side through all the sadness—my mother's death, both of our fathers' deaths, my brother's and Mania's mistreatment, everything.

The wind now feels welcome, beating against my heated face. I pull out the loaf of bread that Jozef gave me. It is cold and dry, but at least it will fill my stomach.

"Stella."

My eyes open, a string of saliva dripping from my lips to Andrzejek's shoulder. I pull back, my hand flying to my drooping cheek.

Oliwjer smiles. "You slept well then?"

Andrzejek tilts his head, casting a reprimanding glance at his brother. "We are here, Stella," he says, turning to me.

I stare down to my lap and realize I am still holding the frozen loaf in my hand. I wrap it up and climb down the side of the cart. The two boys are already a step ahead of me, unloading my cart. They pull it to me, and Oliwjer shakes his head in disbelief.

"Your brother expects too much of you. This cart is heavy for me to pull twelve miles, let alone a girl. Stella, you deserve better than Jozef and Mania."

I shrug. I have heard this often, but I never know what it means. Does anybody really deserve anything?

Andrzejek leans down, hugging me softly. "Promise me you will be careful."

I nod, squeezing my arms around his neck. "Thank you."

Oliwjer's eyes narrow as he looks at the road ahead. It seems forgotten, not a single soul or mule along the path. "Are you sure you can do this, Stella? I can go with you, if you'd like."

I shake my head, my shoulders falling. "It looks worse than it is. By the time you are finished working, I will be sitting at Amalia's table, a plate of sweet bread in front of me."

Andrzejek presses his lips together, the lines around his eyes deepening. "As you say, Stella." I know he wishes to say more, but he doesn't. He knows me too well.

I swallow, nodding.

Oliwjer places his hand on my shoulder. "Watch for rocks. It is easy to stumble when you are already weary."

And then they are gone. I stand beside the cart, watching as their wagon rolls out of sight, back the way it came.

Five more miles; then four, three, and two, until finally I reach the road leading into Ostroleka.

I am beginning to think I was wrong about the first mile being the most difficult; maybe it is the last. The remaining steps feel like an entirely new mountain I must climb. My arms are numb. They feel neither the strain nor the cold. But my legs do. They feel every last incline of the lane, each stony ridge that the cart must navigate, and every last excruciating step.

At last, I round the last corner. I see Amalia's home, positioned perfectly between the neat row of homes. The ground is only slightly covered in snow, as most of it has blown over into drifts along the houses and bushes.

Like everywhere else in Poland, times have been difficult here. The factories, much like the farming my brother does, pay little. People are beginning to anger. Some have even started to strike, demanding better pay. I do not blame them, but they are not wise. The workers cannot win. Factories will only bring in cheaper labor like the Croatians, like Mania's father.

I pass a few Russian officers in the lane. They stare at me in disdain. We are part of the Russian empire, they say. But I know better. We will never be anything but Polish. To them, we are just an addition, a workhorse for their field.

Three

Kto dwa zające goni, żadnego nie złapie.
Grasp all, lose all.

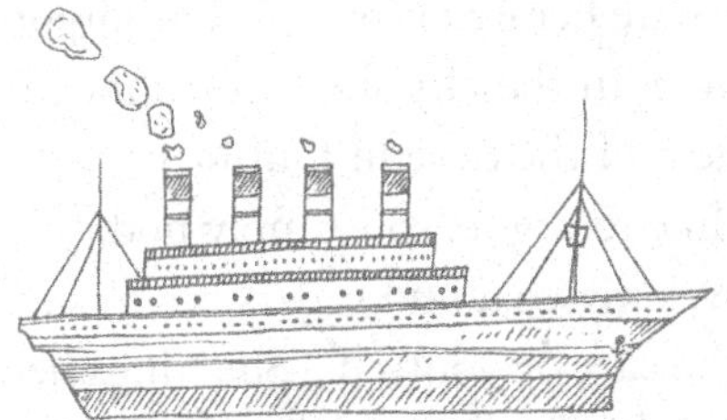

The smell of warm bread fills the entryway of Amalia's home. I can almost taste the walnut and cinnamon. Her two youngest boys run when they hear my name. Dawid, the larger of the two, nearly knocks me over as he reaches my arms.

"Ciocia Stefania! You have come!" he yells, jumping up and down.

Kamil, the youngest, stops short of the door, hesitantly holding onto a small rag blanket. He has always been shy. I hold out my arms to him, but he retreats toward Amalia, frantically whispering, "Matka. Matka."

His voice is sweet, and I cannot help but love Kamil for his gentle way.

Dawid pulls at my hands. "How long will you stay?"

Amalia finds her way to me, pushing past the mess of the room. She hugs me. "Stefania, how are you?" she asks, but her observant nature has already found the answer. She grasps my cold fingers into her own, her eyes filling with concern. She peers around the doorframe at the cart near the steps. "Have you come alone this time? Where is Jozef?"

I shake my head. "His leg is giving him trouble. He is also worried about Bronia."

"The little one is still not better?" my sister asks, surprised.

"No, she still coughs. We worry it has reached her lungs." I shrug as I say it. I have not even wanted to admit the fact to myself.

"Surely Jozef should have brought Bronia here to the doctor," Amalia says, irritation overriding her concern. Her hand is placed against her hip, and for a moment I imagine her as my own mother, worried for my safety, angry for the thoughtlessness of others.

But I cannot share her irritation. She has forgotten how hard our living really is. Here, in the city she is surrounded by conveniences. We go without most of the time in Durliosy.

But I do not like to argue, so I simply nod.

Amalia removes my coat and orders me to sit. "I cannot believe you have pulled the cart by yourself." She flings her hands in the air. Her dark hair is pulled back into a bun and shimmers in the sunlight. Her complexion is clear. She is beautiful.

"The cart should be much lighter on the way home," I say. I smile, remembering Andrzejek and Oliwjer. "And it was not as bad as it could have been. At least I was away from Mania."

Amalia's eyes glisten, a shared secret shining back at me. She knows how Mania treats me, how my brother uses me for labor. But Amalia does not know how to help me. Still, she tries.

"Stefania, if you were to marry—" she begins.

I raise my hand in protest. Not today. I have never been one to take advice well, but exhaustion exacerbates the worst in me; I am not sure I can control my tongue. It is better that we do not discuss it.

Amalia has offered to have me stay with her in the city, until I secure a husband. Many of the immigrants and workers are without a wife, or even a friend. It is hard labor, and Amalia says that I could have my choice of the men. They need someone to cook for them and take care of them. Sixteen, she says, is not so very young.

But I have spent my entire childhood taking care of others—Casimir and Jozef, Bronia, and even my brother and Mania. Yet there is no one to take care of me. Sometimes I like that. Other times, I wish it were different.

If I marry, it will not be to escape Mania and Jozef.

"I have written to Wiktor again," I say, awaiting her disapproval.

"Yes?" Amalia asks, only partially focused as she busies herself around the stove. "And have you heard how he is, how Stanislaus is?"

My American brothers have been a sore topic for too long. Amalia feels they have abandoned us. I swallow, trying to bury the hope that comes each time I think of joining them. "It seems the work is good there. Wiktor says he is not so poor as we are here. The city of Baltimore is alive, and Wiktor promises to help me get there." I take a piece of potica and bite it, aware of what is to follow.

But Amalia is quiet.

After a moment, I look up and find tears in her eyes. "Stefania, Wiktor will never be able to come back to take you to America, and you cannot travel it alone, a young girl. It is not safe, and even more than that, it is not what Father would have wanted."

A lump forms at the base of my throat. I blink away a few tears of my own. Then the anger comes, like a gust of wind—suddenly and forcefully. "You think I am old enough to be married off, yet you do not believe I could make the journey on my own? And why does it matter what Father would have wanted? He is the one that truly abandoned us, dying in a fight he had no chance of winning. He hated the way the landowners treat us. He hated the soldiers. He wanted an independent state. Just look where it got him and us."

Amalia's hands fly to her hips once more, and she tosses the rag in her hand. I see the rigidness of her stance, the stubbornness embedded in her brow. "You must not speak like that. Father was mistaken, yes, but he loved this land. He only wanted to make it better." Her voice drops on the last words, and I sense her pain.

I know she misses our father more than I do. She remembers him better. She remembers goodness. I only remember what he left me: nothing. I feel the bitterness swell inside of me each time I think of him, and it scares me.

Amalia reaches out to touch my hand, her soft skin against my coarseness. "I do not want you to go."

The fire inside my chest breaks for a moment, and then dissipates when I meet her gaze. Amalia cares for me. My sister is the only person that has lived through what I have.

I straighten my shoulders, brushing my hand across my dirty dress. “I do not think you need worry about it. I will never have the money to leave, and I know I cannot count on Wiktor. He has not changed that much.” I hear the disappointment in my own voice, feel the tears prickling my eyes.

This seems to satisfy Amalia, and she places her hand on my arm, leaning her head closer. “Perhaps you will marry Andrzejek.”

I close my eyes, feeling a new pain in my heart. “Maybe,” I say, knowing it will never be. Perhaps if things were different.

Four

Kto buja wysoko, bywa próżny.

It is not the cow that shouts the loudest that gives the most milk.

Men file by my cart, shoulders bumping into one another as they struggle to get through. The market always seems busy, and today is no different. The crowds overwhelm me. Ostroleka has become a trading center for the province, and the Russian military camp has only added to the size.

The guards patrol the streets because of the proximity to the Prussian border, checking the merchants' licenses to sell. But everyone knows that the soldiers are really searching for any indication of rebellion, especially from the Jews. The czar puts more restrictions on them each time I visit. First the Jews were banned from wearing their religious clothing, and now only those deemed useful are allowed to sell at market, live in the village, or attend school.

It frightens me—the power of the czar. It might be the Jews that the Russians hurt most, but I know the soldiers do not like Polish villagers like me much more.

A woman across from me yells above the noise, "Breads for sale!"

The shrill voice awakens me to my surroundings.

"It is always so before the winter sets in," the man selling wool beside me says. His gray hair is wavy, wisps falling out and around his dark cap.

I stare, but say nothing.

"The crowds and noise. The people are preparing for the cold. They can feel it is coming," he says, rolling a cigarette.

I nod, my gaze falling in front of me. I've never been good at speaking to strangers.

"You are young." His voice cracks.

I turn to him once more, my eyes meeting his light blue ones.

"And alone," he adds, raising a brow.

I hear only kindness in his words, so I nod. "Yes," I begin. "My brother could not come with me this time."

A sudden breeze carries the aroma of sweet breads, the smell almost overwhelming my aching stomach. I absentmindedly lick my lips.

The man shakes his head, spitting between puffs of smoke. His eyes are fixed on me. "You are hungry."

I shake my head. "I have enough."

I turn back to my cart, hoping I will sell the goods before long. The pain of yesterday's exertion has made its claim, and I struggle to stand, to keep from crying out. My hands are red and swollen; large blisters cover my palms and the skin between each finger.

The eggs and milk sell quickly. But because I am a girl, many try to take advantage of me, assuming I know nothing of business. I do not read or write well, but I know all about money. Or better yet, the lack of it. I am firm, and some turn away, disgusted at my prices. But they come back. There is little milk in the city. Eggs are not so easy to come by either, and so they may crinkle their brows when they hand me their coins, but they hand me their coins.

Ofttimes, the faces blend together, the colors and features from one person melding into the next. That is how the languages feel too. Polish is clearest, and thanks to Mania's commands, Croatian comes second. But the most difficult is Russian. Perhaps it is because I do not try so hard with that language. It feels forced, and if I am honest, it is forced.

A Croatian man stands in front of me. His unkept hair falls around dark features and a prominent nose. His brows are knit together, dirt lines patterning after the wrinkles along his forehead. His hands are thick, strong, and most pronounced—dirty. His ebony eyes scan my own as he inspects the bottles of milk.

"How much?" he asks.

"Nine grosze," I say, almost double of what I charged the others.

He sets the bottle down in response, his eyes narrowing. "Nine grosze?" he asks, tilting his head. He meets my gaze and asks the price again.

For a moment I cannot speak. It's as if this man can see through me, and his clenched fists unnerve me. I clear my throat. "Seven grosze," I say, fidgeting with my hands.

He holds his hand out and drops the coins into my hand.

I nod and smile, handing him the bottle.

But my breath catches. There is something about his eyes that unnerve me. His gaze is dark and fierce, but I cannot look away. His eyes remind me of icicles—cold and unforgiving. They tell a story of survival, and for a moment I regret charging him the higher price, knowing he is just as desperate as I am. Perhaps more.

But he leaves, disappearing into the throngs. Then another customer comes, and I seem to forget him.

I sell the remaining goods, except for a few heads of cabbage, then pack my stool into the cart beside the baskets. Relief washes over me. Jozef will be pleased with my efforts.

"Young woman."

The sound cuts through the air, and I feel my shoulders tighten. I turn again to the old man next to me. "Yes?"

He hesitates, kicking his foot against the dirt. He repositions his cap and he flicks his cigarette to the ground. The small flash of orange light diminishes almost instantly. His eyes meet mine. "I watched you today. You sold well."

I nod, turning away. But I can still feel him beside me.

"I noticed your coat."

My cheeks burn. I am wearing my worn-out coat, too embarrassed to wear Jozef's ill-fitting, warmer one.

He continues, "I had a daughter once. She died years ago, but I suspect she was about your age. Here, take this." He hands me a neatly folded yardage of wool. "You should have a warmer coat."

I am stunned. This is not how we do things in Durliosy. I shake my head, softening my voice, "I am sorry to hear of your daughter, but I cannot take the wool. Your daughter would rather you sell it to feed your family."

He pushes the fabric toward me with more force. "I have no family left. Take it. Promise me you will not sell it. Make a new coat." He shakes his head in dismay. "I do not want anything in return. Just to know I helped someone else's daughter."

This is enough for me. I take it, bowing my head in gratitude. Perhaps there is kindness even in winter. I pull my empty cart to the street with just enough time to find medicine for Bronia.

Five

Kogo Pan Bóg stworzy, tego nie umorzy.
Each day brings its own bread.

The load is lighter and the road is quieter on my journey home. The stillness calms me. The journey will take half the time, cost half the energy. I take my time, periodically stopping to rest, drink, and eat from the food Amalia sent along with me.

I turn back to the neatly folded wool.

It is a dream.

I look at it again and again, as if seeing the wool once more will convince me that it is real. Before market I had wished for a new coat, and now I have the means to make one. This is not the first time something like this has happened.

Maybe wishes are like prayers.

My brother Franz, the parish priest of the village, would tell me that I am wrong. He believes in rituals and the letter of the law. No one can get answers without praying, and even then, Franz says God wants a humble people and does not answer most prayers. I have heard his sermons enough to know my own insignificance. I do not often pray, doubting I will even be heard.

But sometimes God still gives me what I wish for, sometimes still answers the prayer of my heart. This time, He sent wool from a man that was kind.

I pass the halfway mark. I have only been walking for two hours.

I do not know how to explain the wool to Jozef. I am worried he will think I stole it or cheated him. Even if he did believe me, it would not stop Mania from wanting it for herself or for the children.

I do not have many skills, but I am good at hiding things. Once, Mania saw a hairpin that I kept beneath my bed. It belonged to my mother, perhaps the only thing left of her I had. I was twelve years old, and Mania took the hairpin, claiming that I did not know how to appreciate such beauty. I was young, but even then, I knew that it belonged to me.

My mother was kind; Mania is not. My mother was sweet; Mania is bitter. Every good part and memory of my mother seemed to be ripped away with the presence of Mania. But at twelve, I determined not to let Mania take that last piece of my mother from me. I found the hairpin the next day, inside a cup on Mania's shelf, and I hid it. To this day, Mania is angry that she lost it. She blamed me, beating me across the face as punishment.

I cannot let Mania see the wool, but it will be difficult. Unlike the small hairpin that easily slipped inside my apron pocket, the wool is more difficult to conceal. It is thick, good material—the type a girl like me does not own.

I stop, turning to tuck the bundle in the folds of my worn-coat. I will take it to the loft, for my coat truly needs mending.

It feels like something is coming, some wave of change that will transform my life and the people in it. The circumstances of the last two days point to something better, something hopeful. The ride on Andrzejek's cart, the wool, the peaceful journey home—they are signs of better days to come.

I believe it is America.

My talk with Amalia did nothing to ease the unsettling within me. If anything, it strengthened my resolve to leave this sad place. The Croatian man in the market—I cannot forget his eyes. They told a story that I long to be a part of, a story of survival.

In truth, I have not allowed myself to hope like this before. For me, hope has always led to disappointment and bitterness. Yet there is a little voice inside my heart that tells me to trust the signs this time, trust the way I feel I am being pulled.

I pass a bend in the road, spotting the familiar parish. It is a small church, one that holds only the families of the farms outside of Durliosy. I stop the cart, resting it against a large rock. It has been three weeks since I have seen my brother Franz. I have not been to church since Bronia's illness.

I walk the small dirt path that leads to the entrance. The old wooden door is heavy, but I pull it open, the sound of my boots against the soft dirt floor a welcome change from the rocky landscape. There is a candle lit in the corner of the dark room, and I can see Franz's figure.

"Stefania," he says, standing to greet me. He is my brother, yet he views me as a pastor might instead, the look of providential concern, laced with a warning of prudence, gleaming in his eyes.

"Franz, I am just returning from market in Ostroleka." Instantly I feel a great distance between the pair of us. I feel empty around him, like I have lost something. "It has been too long since we spoke."

Franz seems unaware of my discomfort, the way I have to force the words between us.

He sets down the incense, nostrils flaring, and a frown stretches across his pale face. "You are wearing Jozef's coat. Where is yours?" he asks, a hint of concern etched in his brow.

I shake my head, biting the inside of my cheek because it feels strange to speak of anything more than church with Franz. Being by his side reminds me of pulling the cart to Ostroleka. It takes so much effort, and sometimes I am tired at just the thought of trying. But I clear my throat, telling myself to endeavor once more. "Jozef's leg is hurting him. I went to market alone. My coat has holes and is thin, so he lent me his."

Franz gestures for me to follow him to the back room. There, he shows me a pile of donated clothing. "Will you take one of these garments to patch your coat? What I have, I give freely."

"Oh," I say, attempting a smile. I am a member of his congregation, nothing more. I want to cry, but I shake the sadness away.

It is one less person to regret leaving.

I see two pairs of trousers that might be made into a liner for my new coat. I gather them, awaiting my brother's approval. "And what of that dress?" I ask, nervously pointing.

"Would you like it, Stefania?" he asks, tilting his head. "I have no use for it."

I smile, surprised at his response. "Yes, if it is not too much."

Franz grasps my shoulder, wrinkling his brows. His lips purse, and his voice deepens. "Glory be to God. He giveth, and He taketh away."

It takes all my restraint not to turn my head in disgust. Franz tries to talk like a saint. He is a pastor, but he is also my brother—the same brother that used to pull my hair and steal my doll. Yet since he returned a priest some years ago, he speaks differently. He seems to think that the clergy attire gives him respect and authority. He believes it makes him better than he was before.

Maybe it does. But maybe he is still the same boy that used to tease and laugh with me. Maybe he could still be my friend, my brother, and not just a holy man sent to counsel me and rescue my tattered coat.

The dips and turns along the path indicate I have not far to go. The slanted roofline of the house extends past the cluster of trees, and already, I hear the chickens and goats. It must be warmer today, for the animals are much quieter in the cold.

I take the cart to the barn. There is room to hide my treasures beneath the hay—the new wool and trousers, my dress and a couple of coins. Jozef is not observant like some. He has too much on his mind to notice anything other than the animals and his own dinner.

The cart now tucked inside the barn, my shoulders and mind are lighter, and I stand taller, heading for the house in search of Bronia. She must hear my footsteps before I reach the threshold, for I recognize the pattern of her feet against the floorboards, running toward the open door. I step through, welcoming her into my arms.

"Ciocia Stella, you are home," Bronia says, smiling all the way up to her eyes. She rests her head against my shoulder, coughing so hard I can feel her perspiration across my neck.

I stand, pulling her against my hip. "And you should not be running. I thought you were to get better, yes?"

She says nothing, but wraps her arms around my neck instead, squeezing me so tightly that I have to catch my breath.

My brother stands by the table, a look of worry written in the lines of his eyes and lips. I reach into my pocket and toss the money on the table. The coins splatter against it in an almost musical way.

Jozef's eyes widen. He counts them silently, his lips mouthing the numbers. He finishes and looks up at me, confusion and something more—perhaps distrust—marking his brow and narrowed eyes. "Stefania, the medicine? How could you forget?"

I pull the tinctures from my pocket, placing them beside the coins.

Jozef jerks backward in response, his mouth gaping open. He grips the edge of the table, as if it is the only thing keeping him from falling.

I stay still, waiting for him to ask what I know he must.

"But how can this be? How have you purchased the medicine and kept so much of the earnings?"

I rarely find satisfaction with Jozef. He does not compliment me, and this is as close as it gets—astonishment at my ability.

"I traded well, Jozef."

His eyes are fixed on me, his expression suddenly new and undistinguishable.

"Have I done well?" I ask, already aware of the answer, but wanting so badly to hear it. My question hangs like a whisper in the wind—quiet and unanswered.

He falls back into his chair and breathes deep. He only nods, but stops when he sees I am waiting for his reply. Then, his dark features resume their normal rigidness, the astonishment vanishing and replaced with sternness. He brushes his dark thumb across his forehead, pushing aside his wiry hair.

"Did I not say you could do it?" he asks.

I nod, a lump rising in my throat.

"Perhaps I should send you to market every time. You are better at it than I thought you would be."

Six

Serce nie kłamie.
The heart sees farther than the head.

Bronia is much worse, and my heart feels as if it might rip in half—one side in anger, the other in pain. It is hard to see her so sick, so sad.

Mania is angrier than usual. I know it is because she worries about Bronia. Yet instead of ordering me around, Mania surprises me by giving me the responsibility of caring for Bronia, to get her better.

I welcome the task. My body is still exhausted from going to market, the blisters on my hands just beginning to scab over. The boys are to sleep with their parents until Bronia is better. It is only the two of us in the loft for days on end.

Bronia only lays there, her dry cough falling against the silence. Her normally animated expression instead falls flat, her pale lips forming a pursed line and her rosy cheeks dimmed.

I bring boiling pots of water to Bronia's side, letting the steam flow to her lungs. I cover her with blankets, administering the tinctures as often as I can. The cool rag against her burning forehead seems to have no effect, but I keep it there, hoping it will lessen the raging fever that threatens to burn her little body.

There is nothing else I can do but wait and tell stories.

I worry I will run out of stories. Bronia asks for them all day. Sometimes I stop, thinking she has fallen asleep, but she stirs the moment I cease, her hand reaching out for mine, begging me for more. She is so ill and seems so far away that I am beginning to wonder if she is living the stories in her dreams. I make the stories especially sweet, just in case.

The loft affords me time to think, time to consider my options for the future and the present. The late nights watching Bronia also provide more than enough time to sew my new coat. Each night I work on it dutifully, from the moment Bronia drifts to sleep and I can finally rest my voice.

I guard my secrets. I do not mean the lying, scheming type of secrets, but the precious, hopeful, and perhaps even timid ones. It seems my life has been a sequence of disappointments and depressions, as if each time a ray of light is exposed, someone is there to dim it, effectively restoring the darkness that has covered so much of my experiences.

I have learned that if I am to keep anything in life, I must keep a secret.

"Ciocia," Bronia whispers, tugging at my arm, and in turn, interrupting my thoughts.

I pull the blanket over my newly sewn coat, careful not to draw attention to it.

"Bronia-sweet," I reply, tenderly cradling her head to my chest.

"Am I better yet?"

I smile. She asks this each time she wakes. "Not yet, my little one."

Bronia turns her head and shakes, a dry cough escaping into a cloud against the chilling air. Her chest heaves as she breathes in, and I almost worry her lungs will collapse.

"Turn to the steam," I command. I pour more medicine into her mouth.

She swallows, gripping my arm for support. Her skin is paler than yesterday, and I am not convinced the medicine is helping. I tap lightly on her chest, hoping to loosen the grip of whatever has taken her.

"I love you, Ciocia," Bronia says.

I love her too. I tell her.

"But what if I am so sick that I cannot talk to tell you that I love you?" she asks with wide eyes, her forehead scrunching.

I put a finger to her lips and straighten the blanket. I swallow, and with a scratchy voice, I tell her a new story. "Once there was a man who had a daughter he loved very much," I say, stroking her back. "The little girl loved to pick branches of the black birch trees. She used to tell her father that their love was like those branches—strong and sweet for forever. Then one day, the daughter grew sick and died, and the man was broken. He did not know how he could tell her he loved her, and he wanted to reach her once more so he could speak the words again. But she was gone, and he could not speak to her. So, he decided to pick black birch branches and scatter them upon her grave each day. The daughter watched from heaven and knew that her father loved her." I stop, realizing Bronia's coloring has come back a bit.

"But what if I cannot pick black birch branches—what if I am too sick, Ciocia?" Her lips quiver.

My fingers slide to her mouth once more.

She coughs.

"The point of the story is not that you must pick me branches," I say, "but that when two people really love each other, they find their own special way to say it."

Bronia smiles in the way I have come to adore, her nose crinkling and her large brown eyes twinkling. I have not seen that smile for days.

I squeeze her tight. "You look better than you did yesterday, Bronia. I am sure you are getting better."

Seven

Kto się ożeni, to się odmieni.
Marry and grow tame.

Andrzejek catches my eye from across the chapel. Between the dust and motes dancing in the sunlight, I see his hand wave back and forth in attempts to attract my attention. He sits five benches in front of me, but his right arm rests on the back of the pew and his head is fixed on me.

He mouths some phrase, but I can hardly see his lips, let alone the shapes they make. His brows scrunch together as he concentrates his efforts in my direction. The amusement of seeing Andrzejek so animated and exaggerated forces a small laugh from my lips.

"Death comes to everyone. Will you be ready?" Franz asks sternly, his dark eyes scanning the congregation. He pauses, staring directly at me. "When was the last time you went to confession? The last time you fasted?"

I bite the inside of my cheek, trying to forget the humor of Andrzejek's expression. I straighten my back, and the bench creaks in response, cutting the silence around me.

"And when we speak of sacraments . . ."

My brother begins reading scripture, and suddenly his voice seems to fade into the very page he reads from. I cannot read, and at times, my brother's words seem as foreign as the writings on the paper. His drawn-out phrases and monotone are enough to put me to sleep.

Sitting as straight as I can, I pinch my forearms to keep awake. Every effort is worth avoiding Franz's censures. He gave me a stern reproach the last time I drifted off, and I found myself confused, analyzing the situation for days afterward.

Franz is my pastor, more so than my brother. I keep coming to this realization, over and over and over again, as if each Sunday it is a new discovery. Perhaps it is only because I wish things were different between him and me. I hope that a piece of the brother I used to know returns someday, even if I am gone by then.

When the service comes to an end, Mania digs her elbow into my ribs. "Your friend waits to speak to you," she says, bobbing her head as she always does when she is irritated. Her crooked finger points toward Andrzejek, who stands at the end of our pew.

I wrap my scarf and make my way to him.

A flicker of light dances across his eyes when I meet his gaze. The dimples on his cheeks deepen, and his boot taps against the ground.

"Andrze," I say in a soft tone. "You cannot distract me like that. You know how Franz is."

He grins and scratches his head. "About that, I am sorry. It is just that I was hoping you could get away for this afternoon."

"One of our walks again?" I ask, lifting a brow.

He shakes his head. "Something like that. Stella, will you have lunch with me?"

My eyes narrow, and my hand rests on my hip. "What is this about, Andrze?"

"I packed a picnic," he explains, a mischievous smile replacing his excited expression.

I turn to my brother. Jozef is already staring at me in anticipation of my request. He does not say anything, but gives a small nod and grunt. It is at times like this that my brother surprises me.

"Where are we going to have a picnic in this cold weather?" I ask him.

Andrzejek nods. "So you will come?"

I tilt my head, scanning his face for some explanation of his strange manner. "Yes, but will you tell me what is going on?"

He winks, as if that gesture is enough to satisfy my curiosity. Then, he helps me into his wagon. Most of the congregation are like me; they walk. But Andrzejek lives further and often brings surplus to Franz.

"Stella, I have so much to tell you. I do not know where to begin," he says, much too rapidly. He pauses, wiping away a small bead of sweat above his brow.

"Go on, Andrze," I prod, giving him a gentle jab with my elbow.

He grabs the reins and breaks the horses into a gallop. The impact almost sends me tumbling off the seat and into the pile of potatoes behind me. Somehow, my hands grasp the board beneath me and I manage to escape the tumble. I rub the stab of pain in my neck.

"Are you trying to kill me?"

Andrzejek's deep laughter fills the space between us, and he pulls the reins to one side. The wagon turns and slowly skids to a stop beside a rocky ledge.

His refusal to explain anything eats at me, and I click my tongue on the roof of my mouth. It would do no good to push the issue further, so I change the subject, pretending not to notice his strange expression. "Bronia is better. It is a relief," I say through chattering teeth.

"Yes, I saw her at church."

I nod, irritated that he ignored my attempt at conversation.

"Franz's sermon was particularly enlightening today," I say.

I do not even get a reply for this attempt. Andrzejek cocks his head toward me, a brow raised in humor, but he does not say anything. He has told me multiple times he might quit going to church if it was not for Franz being my brother. I sometimes wonder if the same is true for me.

"Where is Oliwjer?" I ask.

"We both thought, given the circumstance, it would be better if I came alone to tell you the news."

"The news?"

Andrzejek smiles, but this time it is kind, calmer.

"Well, out with it!" I say, leaning closer to him.

But he doesn't say anything. Instead, Andrzejek pulls me nearer, his eyes resting on my lips.

For a moment, I lose myself. My heart beats loud against my chest, so loud I can hear it, feel it pulsing through my fingers and toes. The back of my neck burns, the heat making its way to my cheeks.

He leans closer, and I feel his lips meet mine. His kiss is hard, cold, and nothing like what I imagined it would be so many times before. My anticipation is replaced by disappointment and emptiness. He pulls back and surveys my face.

I know he felt it too. It was not right.

"Well?" Andrzejek asks. His eyes are glistening, and his jaw juts forward. "Was it so bad, or was it worth the surprise? We can get better at it with practice."

I pull away, catching my breath. I am sure he noticed my compliance, the way I did not protest in the least. But he must also see the shock.

I cannot meet his eyes, so I look down at my feet and at the horses below instead. "It is so cold, Andrze," I say. "Maybe we should go home."

The silence becomes suffocating, and in a moment of weakness, I dare to look up at his expression.

The damage is done. Andrzejek's eyes betray his disappointment.

I find the courage to grab his hand. It is so much warmer than mine, and I wince at the realization of how good my hand feels in his. "I am only shocked. You have always been only my friend."

Andrzejek's eyes have welled with tears. He pulls his hand from mine and drops his head, catching it in his hands. "Oh, Stella, I knew it was not right. But I hoped things could change. You see, Oliwjer and I have decided to lease the land just north of yours. Oliwjer considered asking you to marry him first—you must know he cares for you—but he said that he thought I stood a better chance." He lifts his head, rubbing his hands together to keep warm. "I just thought if you were away from Jozef and Mania that maybe you would change your mind."

"Change my mind about what?" I ask.

"America."

My mouth falls open, and it takes a moment before I can close it.

"I have this sinking feeling that I will lose you forever," he says. "I know you would rather be a hundred miles from this place. You would wish it forgotten, but you mean too much to me, to Oliwjer. This place, this land, it is a part of you, whether or not you wish it to be. If you stay, I promise Oliwjer and I will make things right."

I am nodding, but I do not know why. I will not agree to stay.

He continues, "I can take care of you, the way you should be taken care of. You will not be far from Bronia."

A few snowflakes are falling now.

Andrzejek knows how I love my niece Bronia. He is a good man, if you can call him that. He is only eighteen. He is kind and giving, but I do not think he loves me. He has never loved me, not in the way that a man should love a woman when he offers for her hand in marriage. I cannot let someone do for me what I have been doing my whole life—sacrificing every part of myself for the welfare of another.

"Andrze," I say, gasping for breath, "You do not want to marry me; you want to save me. I cannot let you give up your heart. I know you care for Lodzia. I've seen the way you look at her and smile."

What I say is true, but I can tell Andrze is still upset. I watch him, waiting for him to reply.

"Stella," he says, his voice cracking. "You cannot leave. I see it on your face. You have as good as decided, but I want you to know that you have another option. You have always been a good girl and done just what was asked of you. You have always been my friend. I want to do this for you. I know we can grow to love each other in that way."

Warm tears are sliding down my face, and I dab the edge of my scarf along my cheeks. I am crying, but I am not sure why. I think it is because I do love Andrzejek. I have loved him my whole life, and I think he knows this.

"Are you going to be stubborn about this?" he asks, flipping the reins. The horses start to walk.

I bite my lip. "Yes. You are right, Andrze. I am going to leave. I do not know how or when yet, but I am going to America."

He nods and sighs, seeming to realize it is no use to push his offer further. "Then will you consider Oliwjer?" he asks.

I laugh, rolling my eyes. "No, Andrze. He is like an older brother to me, a better brother than the ones I have."

He is quiet until he turns down the dirt road by my house. He smiles, a sadness casting a shadow in his gaze. "I am going to help you get there, Stella, if that is what you really want."

I choke back tears. Yes, oh yes. That is what I really want, to leave all this behind me and begin again.

Eight

Dla chcącego nic trudnego.
If there is a will, there is a way.

I pour the steaming pot into the goats' bucket, trying not to burn my fingers in the process. The grass hay is already laid out, but still the oldest goat does not stir. She has not eaten in two days. I do not think she will make it past the winter. She looks miserable, and I worry.

My shovel scrapes against the barn floor, and I pause to catch my breath. If I am honest, it is not the goat that troubles me. The truth is, I have not seen Andrzejek for over two weeks. He has not been to church or by the house. I worry he stays away because of our last meeting.

Shaking my head, I resume work. Andrzejek has never avoided me.

"Stefania!"

Even with my back turned, I know the voice of Jakub Lapat, the boy that delivers the post. This can only mean one thing: Wiktor has written.

I drop my shovel at the realization, anticipation flooding my already weakened body. "Jakub," I say, wishing I had kept the shovel for support.

Moving to the barn opening, I pant like a child. I wipe my face with the edge of my sleeve, noting the streak of dirt along my cuff. Stray hairs fan my face. I must look as anxious as I feel.

He laughs, holding something behind his back.

"What is it, Jakub?" I ask, leaning toward him. "Is it Wiktor? Has he written again?"

He holds his hand up high, revealing a brown parcel. A package.

It is not the package itself that causes my pulse to jump, but rather the possibilities of what it carries, what awaits me. The anticipation is disorienting, like a spinning kaleidoscope at the village festivals.

"Well? Do I have to wrestle you for it?" I ask, trying my best to conceal my impatience.

Jakub smiles. "I wouldn't stop you," he says, reddening.

I stand on my toes to reach it, aware my eagerness has taken over.

He laughs, pushing my hands away. "You know, Stefania, it isn't every day I see packages, especially from America. What do you think it is?"

"I guess I will have to open it to find out," I say, holding out my hands.

Jakub nods, setting the package in my hands, at last finished with his teasing.

"Thank you."

Jakub crosses his arms, and he waits.

I shake my head. "Jakub, thank you for bringing it here."

Jakub cocks his head to the side for a moment, silently surveying me. He grunts, kicking up a small cloud of dirt. "Then you are sending me on my way?" he asks, his freckled face crinkling near his eyes.

I nod. "Yes."

He exhales, jerking his head forward and back. His foot is still sliding back and forth in the dirt. "Right then. I'll be seeing you." He holds one hand up in farewell and then lets himself out the barn gate.

"Until next time," I say, shoulders falling.

Rushing to the corner, I claw at the string and paper until an edge lifts and I can tear it away. A thin brown box. I shake it and hear a tinkling, like marbles . . . or *coins*. Forgetting all manners, I rip apart the box like an animal might.

A small white paper floats to the ground, along with Wiktor's folded letter. There are only a few coins. I bend to gather the papers, finding myself falling to the ground beside them. What do these papers say?

Jozef's heavy footsteps along the dirt startle me, his uneven limp along the wall of the barn. He is coming.

Without thinking, I place the bundle of papers beneath my shirt, the cold coins against my chest, sending a second shock throughout my body.

"Stefania, you are needed in the kitchen."

I nod. It is always so—the chores in the barn, the housework, the children. My days blend together, the difference in tasks being the only separation.

But not today. Wiktor has sent me something—hope. My chest tightens at the thought, aware of the many times I have thought to hope, only to find disappointment instead. I feel the coins against my skin. This time is different, I tell myself. I feel a difference as tangible as the coins against my skin.

Mania stands at the table, hunched above the vegetables. She is trying her hand at stew again. I cringe.

"Stupid girl," she says, gritting her teeth. "Come finish this meal. My back is aching."

A bowl of scrap meat sits to the side of vegetables. It is a mixture of meats, some older than others. Mania gets our meat from a neighbor down the lane in exchange for her mending.

I take the knife from Mania and begin chopping the potato and cabbage.

She squirms into the old rocking chair, her shoulders stooping and her face contorting in pain. Her eyes clench shut, her teeth still gritted and her shoulders tense.

Sometimes I hate her.

Other times I see her misfortune, and I almost forgive how she has treated me. She misses Croatia, she misses the sea, and she misses her family. It can only make matters worse that she battles physical pain too—her injured back from childbirth, her arthritic hands and wrists.

But I struggle to understand why she feels the need to give her pain to me. It would be enough that she suffers. Why must she inflict it upon me as well? If only she had been kinder to me all these years, we might have been friends.

"Why do you stare?" Her dark eyes meet my own. Her jagged teeth rest above her bottom lip, and for a moment she looks as tired as I feel.

I shrug. "You are in pain."

I close my eyes, swallowing hard. Mania does not like me to speak to her.

"You will be too if you do not cook dinner faster."

I wait four more days for Andrzejek.

Nothing.

He misses church again for the third week. I want to go to him, but finding a moment to escape proves difficult. It is only when Jozef leaves to work on a neighbor's property that I leave Mania.

I have kept my papers in the barn with my new coat and dress. It would be a disaster if Jozef and Mania were to find out about my plans, the coins and papers sent by Wiktor. They would never let me leave.

And there is nothing else I want but to go.

The hill in front of me is the last obstacle standing before Andrzejek's house. The matted brown grass is soggy, wet from the melting snow. Small streams of water flow down the hill in all different directions, making trails of mud. My boots are soaked, but I do not even mind cold toes. I have brought the papers with me. I only hope that Andrzejek is here.

The heavy door is cracked open, and Oliwjer carries a pile of dried wood from the porch. "Stella," he calls, raising his arm in greeting. His features are so similar to Andrzejek's.

I smile. He is good to me, just like his brother. "How are things?" I ask.

He bends, dropping the wood into a pile. He pulls the door shut, winking. "Matka is in one of her moods."

I laugh. Oliwjer always makes light of his mother. She has not been well for years, though her poor spirits are nothing when compared to Mania. Mrs. Skala's husband died in the same revolt as my father. I think that is what ties Andrzejek and me together—the pain of losing our fathers.

"Is Andrze around?" I ask, scanning the nearby field.

"No. He went to market the last few weeks, said he had something important to take care of." He stops, biting the inside of his cheek for a moment. "I thought you knew. You two tell each other everything."

I shake my head. "Not everything."

Oliwjer studies my face, brushing the dirt from his hands as he does so. Andrzejek and Oliwjer are not tall, but they are strong. Oliwjer's eyes are greener, his jaw square.

"Do you know when he will be back?" I ask, finally feeling how cold my toes really are.

This time Oliwjer shakes his head. "I cannot say for sure. I thought he would have been back by now, but these things take time."

"What is he doing there?"

Oliwjer shrugs, seemingly reluctant. "It is a wonder he never said anything to you about it. He went to earn money."

"Doing what?" I ask, my eyes widening.

"He sold at the market, and he took double shifts at the turpentine factory for a couple weeks. I told him I could take care of the farm on my own for a spell."

Why the rush to earn so much money? I want to ask. But I don't, pretending it makes sense. I brush my hair back. "I got another letter from Wiktor. I was going to have Andrze read it for me, but I can come back next week. Will you tell him I was looking for him?"

Oliwjer leans an arm against the door, staring down at me. "Stella, I can read. Let me read it for you."

The back of my neck burns, my stomach dropping. Oliwjer knows my secret, but it feels strange, vulnerable even, to confide in him like this.

Oliwjer digs his hands into his trouser pockets, lurching forward. "Well, are you going to hand it here?"

My hand trembles, but I pull the wad of papers from my coat, handing them to Oliwjer. He glances at them, unfolding the letter.

"Let's see. He writes 'Dear Stella, Baltimore is good to me still. I find work at the meat packing plant.'" He stops, scanning the letter. His brows knit together and he jerks backward, continuing. "'I promised you I would help you. And so I am. I have sent your passage from Hamburg to Baltimore. You will join me in America. I can send only these coins, but you will need to buy your train ticket and have thirty dollars at least when you board the ship.'"

The warm tears that begin to fall multiply until they are streaming down my cheeks. My knees give out, and I stumble to the ground. I cannot meet Oliwjer's gaze, so I bury my face in my apron and wipe my dripping nose.

He sits beside me, his arms enveloping me in an embrace. I let him hold me, relishing in the comfort of his arms.

Oliwjer speaks again, a tenderness to his voice I have not known. "There is more, Stella. He has some instructions for you—where you will meet him in Baltimore and what you need for the boat ride."

And so he recites Wiktor's words.

I just cry.

It is going to happen, and I have been too afraid to truly believe it. Somehow Wiktor took care of me, and I will have to find a way to repay him, to thank him.

Hope blossoms in my chest once more. Wishes and prayers are occasionally answered in a big way. Maybe my heart said another prayer without my knowing. Or maybe it is just Wiktor's kindness.

I give up trying to understand. Instead, I just swallow the sadness of this place, the darkness of my past, and breathe in the promise of my future.

Nine

Lepiej pózno, niż wcale.
Better late than never.

"Stefania."

My gaze is fixed to the pail of milk in front of me, my hands to the goat. I pause, forcing myself to acknowledge my brother's presence.

"You are working too hard. Let me milk her," Jozef says, waving a hand toward the goat.

I smile. "I am almost done, then I will clean the stalls, just as you wish."

He is right. I have been more focused. Tasks that used to tire me invigorate me now. I could skip to market if I had to, even with a full cart.

I have been mending on the side for our neighbors in addition to my chores, hoping to make enough money for my journey. The pay is little, but I take what earnings I can get.

"Do not wear yourself too thin," Jozef says. "We still have market day."

I nod, fixed on the rhythmic sound of the milk against the pail.

"Stefania," he says, his deep voice cracking into the stillness.

My hands fall to my knees at the sound of his emotion.

His feet shuffle in the dirt until he is bent before me. "Stefania, you cannot carry on like this forever." He pulls me by the arm with just enough force to lift me to my feet. His eyes are dark, his jaw set. He points toward the house. "Go."

For a moment, I am stock-still. The determined tilt of his brow and the deep set in the lines around his mouth are all the more perplexing to me. Jozef has never seemed to notice how I carry on at all, let alone care about it.

I stumble a few steps, but stop just short of the barn gate. "Why?" I ask, without turning around. "Why care now, after all the years I've worked for you?"

I hear his low grunt above the milk splashing in the bucket. I turn, and when our eyes meet, Jozef's nostrils flare, and he exhales.

He swipes a few strands of auburn hair from his forehead and stands. "Maybe I work you like a mule too much."

The edge of my lips curve into a smile, but my eyes prick with tears. "Maybe you do."

"He will be back soon, Stella," Oliwjer says one day after church.

I stand outside, waiting for Jozef and Mania to finish speaking to Franz. The sun is warm for the late November afternoon, and instead of wrapping my scarf around my shoulders, I hold it in my hands. It has been five weeks since I have seen Andrzejek.

Oliwjer stands beside me, clutching his hat in front of him. He dips his head toward my brother. "It is good you keep it from them."

My shoulders fall. "You do not think that I wrong them?"

Oliwjer's eyes widen for an instant before narrowing into slits. "Wrong them? Stella, how could you wrong them? No, do not say such things. They would never let you leave, never let you stop working for them day in and day out. It would not surprise me if they were to forbid you from marrying just so they could keep you as their help."

I smile. "Only a friend could speak so vehemently in my defense."

He shakes his head. "No, only a fool would say otherwise."

Jozef and Mania walk toward me, Franz at their side. Little Bronia is waving at me, and I smile back. "It has not been all bad. Some days I wonder if I truly deserve less. They took me in, Oliwjer."

He grasps my arm, pulling me closer and lowering his voice. "Stella, you are not made to live a life of debt and misery. You are brave, and you are strong. If I had less to leave, I would beg to go with you."

I love Bronia and Amalia, Andrzejek and Oliwjer.

But still, I will leave.

Another week passes, and I am sick with worry for Andrzejek. I am only relieved one morning, when I am gathering eggs, and I see his outline riding towards the house. He draws near, and he is out of breath, so much so that he almost stumbles off his horse.

"Stella," he says, his eyes lighting. "Can I speak with you—perhaps one of our walks?"

My sister-in-law stands near the open door, waiting for my basket of eggs. She puffs at the sight of my friend, rolling her black eyes.

I hand Mania the eggs, but do not meet her gaze. "Yes, let's go, Andrze."

Mania saunters toward him, lifting her chin. "Please, take the silly girl off my hands, Andrzejek, but not so long. There is washing and mending to be done."

He sneers at this, and I recognize his angry expression. His cheeks redden, his jaw clenches, and the light in his eyes disappears.

Once past the barn, he grabs my hand and pulls me into an embrace, just as he did when we were children. "It is good to see you."

I wrap my arms around his neck and try to ignore the tingling sensation his hands around my waist elicit. "Where have you been, Andrze? And why did you leave without a single word?"

"Stella," he says, grabbing my hands again. "I have missed you. I have so much to tell you, but Oliwjer says you have something to tell me." He stops, staring at me for a moment. "You look different."

"I feel different," I say, smiling. It takes all my effort not to glance at his hands holding mine, to lean against him.

He laughs, and I can feel his diaphragm move in and out. "Yes?"

"Andrze, it has finally happened. Wiktor has sent my passage to America."

His smile vanishes and he falls back a step, dropping my hands. "Already?"

I bite my lip and tug at a strand of hair beside my face. "Yes, weeks ago, when you were at the turpentine factory."

He crosses his arms. "So, you have everything worked out then?"

He could not have expected this much, at least not so soon. I nod, swallowing the cold air around me. "I still have money to save to get the train ticket and for some of the journey, but I am mending on the side. I am saving, and I have made a new coat," I say, touching his arm.

"Hmm," he says, his voice falling. "Then it is really happening? I am to say goodbye to my dearest friend?"

I do not ever want to say goodbye to Andrzejek. I pretend not to see the emotion in his eyes, the way his lip trembles. "And what have you to say to me? What is your news?"

Andrzejek's brows rise, and he chuckles once more, though in a sad sort of way. "I have another piece of your passage," he says, pulling out a purse from his pocket. "I have worked the past month doing double shifts to earn for your travels. I was prepared to do it even longer, but I do not think that will be necessary anymore."

He pours the contents of the pouch into my hands. It is more money that I have ever seen at once—enough for my journey, enough for the train.

My heart drops. "Andrze, I cannot take this. You have worked too hard for me."

He closes my hand around the purse and money, silencing me. "Stella, it will not be long until you are gone, far away to a place that I can hardly even imagine. But you will always be a part of this place to me. I only want to be a part of where you are going," he says, and I see the tears pooling in his eyes.

"Andrze," I say, shaking my head back and forth. "You are a part of something so much more—my heart." My voice breaks, the catch of a muffled sob silencing me.

He smiles that way I have come to love, where his cheeks rise straight up to his eyes, his lashes tangling together. He kisses my forehead, holding me close. “Then we are even.”

Ten

Kto czeka, ten się doczeka.
He that can have patience can have what he will.

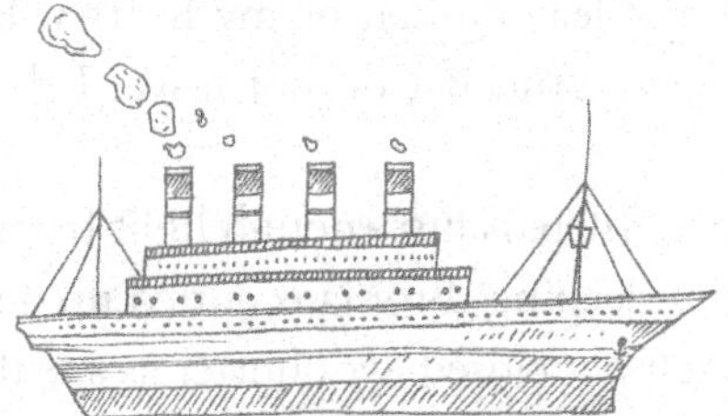

My bag is already packed and hidden beneath a crate in the corner of the barn. All of my new things—my dress and stockings, my coat and mittens, my money, my tickets, the letters from Wiktor, my mother's hairpin, my passport and papers, and a book of my father's—are there. I packed everything a week ago, and I cannot stop checking to make sure it is there each night. I worry little Jozef or Casimir will find it, perhaps Jozef when he cleans the stalls.

But it is still there, waiting for me.

I leave this morning, in the early hours when it is still dark. Andrzejek has promised to meet me at the church. He will ride with me to the train station in Ostroleka. He is giving up a day's work for me again.

I am not going to say goodbye—not to Franz, not to Jozef, and certainly not to Mania. I used to think that blood tied you to someone, but the more I live, the more I see that it is something else entirely.

Mania has been miserable and mean, Jozef unfeeling and relentless. Maybe they needed me. Maybe even Mania, despite all her stabbing words and physical jabs, needed me. She does not know how to survive the pain of life. I almost started to believe that I couldn't either, but then came hope.

I long to leave this past, the pain.

I try not to think of Bronia. She will miss me, but not nearly as much as I will miss her. She has been my star in this darkness. I ache when I think of what will happen when she understands that I am gone for good. I hope she will not be angry. I know she has felt my love.

This will be my only regret—that I cannot take her with me. I cannot think more of leaving her, or my heart will break. And if I break, I will not leave. And if I do not leave, I do not think I can survive.

The loft is quiet. There is just enough light from the moon that I can see the children sleeping. Bronia is curled up next to me. I listen to her breaths, watch her closed eyes flutter as she dreams. Her dark hair is knotted all around the blanket, her hands folded beneath her perfectly round cheeks.

I reach deep into my pockets to find what I put there earlier. The birch branches.

Bending down, I place them in a pattern on the wood floor—a heart. I hope she will remember my story, remember my love. It is the only way I can think to tell her I love her when I cannot speak it.

I climb down the loft with more care than ever before, willing my feet and hands to work together, hoping I will not rock the rickety ladder or shake the floorboards of the loft. I cannot afford a misstep.

Relief washes over me when I reach the bottom. I sigh. Looking around the small house this last time, my eyes fix upon the stove where I spent most nights cleaning, the table that never held enough food to fill my body, and Jozef and Mania's curtain.

I do not think these memories will ever fade, but I wish they would. My eyes fill with tears, my lip quivering in the near darkness. However hard times have been, this home and life has been all I have known.

The bed behind that curtain was where my mother took her last breath. The table that I touch was where I last sat with my father.

But all of it is now part of my past, not my future.

I open the door, commanding myself not to look back. Franz has told me the story of Lot and Sodom and Gomorrah. When he and his family were commanded to leave, his wife looked back, and she was turned to a pillar of salt.

I will not miss this home like Lot's wife. But I think if I look back again, I may turn to stone.

My bag and belongings lay untouched, tucked neatly under the wooden crate.

The animals seem to call to me, telling me to hurry. I pat the goats and smile at the chickens. *Goodbye, friends.*

It is a challenge to find the small lane without the sun, but I am thankful, for once, for the darkness. It is better that I leave here the way I came.

Two miles go by quickly, and I wonder if it is the thrill coursing through my veins or the hope in my hop that propels me farther faster. The sun is just rising as I reach the church, coloring the clouds purples and blues against the golden light. I spot Andrzejek at the next bend, waiting with two horses.

I cannot help myself. I run down the gravel road, forgetting all restraint. By the time I reach Andrzejek, I am bright red from the exercise, laughing in relief.

"You made it," he says, lifting me in an embrace. He swings me around one time, then releases me.

"I did." I hand him my bag, and he ties it on the back of his horse. "Thank you, Andrze. I would not be leaving here today without your help."

He tightens the straps in silence. His jaw is clenched, and I watch the familiar lines of muscle strain as he attempts to smile.

I do not want to say goodbye to him.

As if he can read my thoughts, he flinches and shakes his head. He holds out his hand, helping me to mount the horse. "Do you think I would let you leave any other way?"

Footsteps along the path startle me, and I hear a familiar voice.

"Stefania! Stefania! What are you doing at this hour?"

Franz runs toward us. He wears his night clothes, along with an agitated expression.

I look to Andrzejek, my head swirling around itself. A surge of nausea encompasses me, and my hand instinctively flies to my stomach.

Andrzejek tilts his head and spits to the side. "Do not let him bully you," he whispers.

I spent the last weeks worrying about making it to the train station in Ostroleka unseen, but Franz was the last person I thought would discover my plan.

"Stefania, answer me," he yells, his footsteps growing louder.

"Do you want to leave? We can outrun him," Andzrejek says.

I shake my head, knowing I must face this.

Franz is only feet from my horse now. His face is red from running, his eyes widened. "Well, sister, where are you going at an hour such as this?"

His condescension is irritating, and somehow it gives me courage. "I am leaving, Franz. I am going to America to join Wiktor." The words sound icy, as if I am without feeling.

Franz bends at the hip, his cheeks red from running. He motions toward the church and toward our farm as he tries to catch his breath. "You cannot leave your home, Stefania. You cannot leave Jozef, Mania, the children."

He looks just like Jozef when he is upset, a vein in the center of his forehead splitting like a siphoned river.

"Franz, I do not expect you to understand, but I am leaving. There is nothing left for me here." I fidget with the reins, tempted to run away.

Franz turns. "Andrze? You are a part of this?" When he receives no answers, he pivots back to me. "Stefania, I am advising you not only as you brother and kin, but also as your priest. It is your duty to remain here with your family. It is not right for a girl to leave her family. You are not more than a child."

Andrzejek shifts his weight back and forth on the horse, staring alternatively from me to my brother. "She has made her choice, Franz. Will you wish her well on her journey?"

Franz scoffs at this, shaking his head back and forth. "It is not honest, Stefania, to leave in the dark hours. You should at least have the strength to tell them what you are doing."

"I do not have to answer to them anymore, just as I do not have to answer to you," I say in a broken whisper.

Franz cocks his head back. "And what about God? Do you answer to Him? Does God know what you are doing? Have you told Him?" He stands erect, his arms up in the air, like he is preaching one of his sermons on Sunday.

Andrzejek holds his hand out, placing it on mine. "You do not have to answer him. You do not have to answer to anyone but yourself and God."

Franz is still looking up at me, his face now red out of anger instead of exertion. "Stefania?" he asks, "What will you say?"

I watch my brother for a moment, taking in this last and final memory. My eyes follow the lines around his own, the divots by his chin, and the freckles on his cheeks. I smile despite the sadness I feel. It is so much worse to part like this.

"Franz, God knows my heart." I pause, breathing in the cold air, and I feel my voice crack as I add my final words. "Send my love to Bronia."

I signal to Andrzejek, and we break into a gallop. This time, I do not even wish to look back.

We ride side by side for a couple hours, Andrzejek and me. It is not long until the sun has passed the horizon, lighting the frosted hills and rocky paths. I wish I could make this beautiful landscape my last memory of this place, but I know saying goodbye to Andrzejek will burn brighter in my mind than any view or beauty.

We come to a creek, and the horses stop to drink. We allow them to rest for a moment, feeding on the cold blades of grass that are still growing by the water.

This is not natural for me, saying goodbye. I think if neither of us say it, it won't really happen.

"Stella, you were not meant for this life," Andrze says.

"What do you mean?"

"You are like the star that falls from the sky. You do not belong here on this cold ground."

"That is why you helped me then?" I ask, confused.

"No," Andrze says without hesitation. "I help you because it is what you want. I also trust you. I think you will find your happiness there."

I can see Amalia's house. The train station is just past the turpentine factory. I blow one last birch branch in her direction. Maybe my sister will feel my love as she wakes. She will be feeding her boys soon, sending her stepchildren out the door to the factory. She will not even know I have been here.

Andrzejek clears his throat. "Can we walk the horses the rest of the way?"

I smile. "Of course."

I wish I would have saved a branch for him. But then again, the branches in my story were given when the man was not able to speak with his daughter. I am here, alone with Andrzejek. I can say what I wish. Maybe I should tell him that I do love him, that I would have married him had things been different. It would feel good to tell him the truth before I leave forever.

"There is something I have needed to tell you, but I have not had the courage."

His voice startles me. I turn, blood rushing to my cheeks.

He continues, "I have thought about what you said that day after the church service, when we were in the wagon and I asked you to marry me. You said you did not think I loved you, that I cared for Lodzia—"

I stop him, placing my hand on his arm. "Andrze, I was a fool to say it. I cannot know your heart, only my own—"

He interrupts me. "But you do, Stella. You know me better than I know myself sometimes. I do care for Lodzia. I am not sure why I had not recognized it myself, but I always have. I think I wanted to love you because I saw how much you deserved to be loved."

That word again. Do I deserve anything?

He shifts his weight, reddening as he continues. "I asked for Lodzia's hand two days ago. She has accepted me. We will marry in a month."

My head lurches forward, and I gasp for breath. I turn from him and close my eyes, hoping the emotion choking me will not make its way to tears. Once recovered, I face him, forcing a smile. "Andrze, I am happy for you. She will make a good wife, and you will be good to her, as you have been to me. I cannot wish for more. To know you are happy here will be a comfort."

The whistle of the train sounds, and the wind picks up. Strands of hair are blowing across my face, and I have to stop to push them away. The tracks are only yards away.

"Do you want me to wait with you?" Andrzejek asks.

I shake my head. "I will be alright. You have so much to get back to. Please know I will remember you often—all you have done to help me. You have been better than a friend to me—a brother, a father. Thank you for being the one person to take care of me," I say, handing him my reins.

I worried I would cry, but after the ride and heartbreak, I am not sure I can feel anything now. If I do, I do not think my tears will ever stop.

Andrzejek stops me, placing both hands on my shoulders. He holds me out, giving me a final glance. He shakes his head, sorrow building behind his soft eyes. "Stella Marzewska, you are too much for this sad land. Go, and find the place that you can call home. I will always be here, praying you forward in your journey."

I fall into his arms, but it is not in emotion that I collapse. Rather, it is in urgency. It is time to go our own ways.

He puts some food from his sack into my bag. "For your journey."

We give each other a final goodbye and smile, and then he turns and walks away.

I watch him. He walks on and on, until I can barely make out his gray form against the morning light. Then I can see he has climbed his horse, for two horses run into the shadows.

Eleven

Lepiej umrzeć stojąc niż żyć na kolanach.
It is better to die standing than to live on your knees.

Hope. Heartache. Uncertainty. The train comes to a stop, screeching against the track. A cloud of smoke encompasses me, and I tremble. The moment has come, and for all the waiting and hoping I have done, it still feels sudden. Perhaps such a sensation always accompanies a decision of change. But I am ill, the sensation flooding my chest and head. Hope. Heartache. Uncertainty. I do not know what truly lies before me.

The conductor towers over me.

I force myself forward and hand him my ticket.

"All the way to Hamburg?" he asks without meeting my gaze.

I nod, and he punches a hole in my ticket. He reaches for the next.

My legs shake, but they carry me up the metal steps.

Filing past the slatted benches, I sit near the back. The booth is empty, and I sigh in relief, untying the scarf from my head. The wind howls against the window. I press my fingers to it, watching below.

Faces and farewells, words and embraces—the picture of those beyond the glass stirs me. I pull back, glancing around the compartment. There is no one here to see me go, no one begging me to stay. Andrzejek would have stayed, and he did wish me to stay, but he is gone. I am alone.

The whistle sounds and the train lurches forward, my heart leaping after it. The wheels spin beneath my feet, and the railcar races as fast as my beating heart. This train is unlike anything I know, and it leads me to an even greater unknown.

I lean forward and look out my window once more, watching the town behind get smaller and smaller. Soon there are no houses or farms to see, only the sprawling country and the wintery frost and drifts that line the tracks.

I have already left it behind. *Don't look back anymore,* I tell myself. *Don't turn around.*

The setting sun glares across the glass. I rouse, rubbing the back of my neck and glancing around the railcar. My stomach grumbles, and I reach for my bag.

"Do you have a long way to go?" The woman across from me asks. A baby squirms in her arms, reaching for the strand of hair resting across her cheek.

"Yes," I say, pulling out the bread Andrzejek sent.

She sighs. "The train is hard travel. I hope my baby will not bother you. He is tired but cannot seem to fall asleep."

I smile. "I do not mind. I know how children are."

"I see. I picked the right bench to sit at. I am Marja," she says. A smile stretches across her lips. She cannot be much older than Amalia.

"Stefania," is all I say in return, distracted by two boys across the aisle.

The boys, only a few years older than me, whisper and point. The taller one catches my gaze. His worn-out coat reminds me of my old one.

He stirs when our eyes meet. He grins and turns to his friend. "Should I talk to her?"

My cheeks burn, and I cross my arms.

They laugh.

Anger flares amidst my embarrassment.

"Go, Petar," the other boy says, urging the taller forward.

I turn away, pretending not to notice Petar take the seat beside me. The slats of the bench creak, and he leans closer.

"Miss." His voice shakes. "I could not help but notice you are traveling alone. What is your name?"

I count the trees that pass, determined to remain silent.

Marja shifts her weight, clearing her throat.

"I told you she wouldn't talk to you!" the other boy shouts.

Petar tries again. "This ride would be much more enjoyable were you to talk to me. I am riding all the way to Hamburg. It would be nice to have a pretty face to talk to."

No one has spoken to me like this. The jeering from the other boy grows louder, and my face floods with heat.

"Ah, Petar, forget the girl. There is no fun to her. Come back before she bites you!" the boy from across the booth yells.

My eyes flicker across the aisle.

"Will you at least tell me your name, girl?" Petar asks, repositioning his cap.

"Enough," Marja says, chiding him as only a mother can. She cradles the baby closer. "She does not like this attention. Return to your seat before you wake my babe." She extends a hand, warding him away.

The boy beside me sighs. His shoulders slump forward, and he slaps his hat against his knee. But he stands, relieving me of confrontation.

My face still burns, and I struggle to steady my breaths. I do not even know how to silence a taunting boy. Perhaps I am ill-prepared for what lies ahead.

I fiddle with my bag, trying to find a way to thank Marja.

She speaks before I do. "Those boys have no manners." She clicks her tongue, shaking her head. "You have not traveled much?"

I meet her gaze, clearing my throat. "Not this far."

"I can tell, and so can they. You cannot be so easily affected," she says flicking her chin toward the boys. "Hold your head high, keep your gaze straight, and ignore them. Do not be afraid to yell at them. Some might laugh at you, but it will get the silly ones to leave you alone."

I nod. "Thank you."

She purses her lips, studying me closer. "And Stefania, you should wear your hair back behind the scarf."

"Cover my hair with the scarf—why?" I ask.

Marja smiles. "You are pretty."

I take a bite of bread. *Pretty?* No one has ever called me pretty.

"The scarf will help you to blend in." She stares down at her baby, stroking the few tufts of hair. She glances up, startling when she detects my confusion. "Yes, Stefania, pretty, though not the kind you see every day, which is why it makes you all the more striking. I've never seen hair quite your color—the mixture of reds, browns, and even some blonde; it's lovely with your dark eyes."

My hand instinctively flies to my head, pulling at the strands of hair. It is the only thing besides the hairpin that my mother left me.

"Now, you cannot hide your face wherever you go, but you can hide your hair. You'll want to blend in if you are alone. Sometimes even if you are not alone. Look for someone you can trust, and stay by them," Marja says.

"Thank you," I say once more, managing a smile.

I wish I knew why she was traveling alone. Marja reminds me of the old man at market, the one who gave me wool for a new coat. I never knew strangers could be so kind.

I had not planned on making any friends along the way. It has always been America I see as the journey—freedom and the possibility of a future beyond servitude—but it is quickly becoming clear that there is much ahead of me before that end.

I run my fingers through my hair, pulling it into a tighter knot at the top of my head

Marja smiles and nods.

"Thank you. You are right; I have not traveled at all. I have never been past Ostroleka, and no one talks to me like that in Durliosy."

Marja laughs at this, her eyes gleaming. "I do not know Durliosy, but I am sure that will not be your last encounter with swooning boys. The boys of the big cities have even less manners. You will not blend in, and you are not used to the busyness or the brutality. You are an innocent. That is the type of girl that boys like to tease the most."

I nod, pretending to understand, though I do not think I am innocent. *Do the innocent suffer as I have suffered? Are they worked and mistreated?* I have felt pain and sorrow, probably as much, if not more, than most. I close my eyes quickly, hoping Marja does not see the lone tear roll down my face.

"I only mean innocent when it comes to men," she says, leaning forward to touch my arm.

I flash her a quick smile and turn back to the window. "Yes, I have no experience with them."

"Perhaps I will rest now that the baby is fast asleep," Marja says, leaning her head against the back of the seat. She props her small bag beneath her elbow to support the weight of the baby in her arms and drifts to sleep almost as quickly as the sun sets behind the horizon.

It takes me much longer to fall asleep. It isn't until the other passengers' laughter and speech dies down that the sounds of the train overtake my thoughts and my eyes finally flutter closed. The night sky is dark, and I can almost imagine life back in Durliosy—the loft with Bronia, the wool blankets covering my cold body.

Somehow, I sleep.

Muddled dreams and stiff boards are anything but restful. The train screeches to a stop in Hamburg, and I let out a shaky breath. Another step, another unknown.

Marja was gone when I awoke today, her empty seat a reminder of all that happened yesterday and all that I am unprepared for. I gather my bag, tie the scarf around my head, and step down the steps of the railcar.

Ships of all sizes and colors line the port, spanning as far as I can see. The sails, like white clouds against the sky, stand in stark contrast to the murky and gray water. I lean against a guardrail, watching as a ship departs. Puffs of smoke trail the vessel, the only remnant of its passing. Like the boat, I wonder what follows me, what evidence of my passing, if at all, exists in Durliosy.

Everything is busy; everyone is noisy. Tram cars roll and stop along the streets, dinging and departing in all directions. Buildings tower on each side—buildings that reach high up into the sky, five or six floors high. The copper rooflines come to a point, and many have balconies and railings, arched windows, and stone facades. The craftsmanship is far superior than those of Durliosy or even Ostroleka, and it is warmer here. The winter has not yet come.

A carriage rolls past me, and the horses obediently follow the line of wagons. I clutch my bag to my chest, moving from side to side to avoid the passersby.

There are whistles and shouts, the constant sound of conversation and clamoring along the crowded streets. Unlike the dreariness of Ostroleka, Hamburg is alive with movement, freedom, and, dare I say it, hope.

What did my brothers Wiktor and Stanislaus experience when they stepped off the train? Did they taste the sea and feel the dirt settle on their skin? Did they wander the streets, stopping to see how differently people live here?

Rows upon rows of buildings and steeples surround me, and there is no telling where the city and houses meet—buildings of stacked homes atop businesses and churches aside pubs. Like stacks of hay in a barn, everyone and everything is crowded, competing for space.

It is a wonder I see it with the onslaught of sights and sounds. But the building calls to me, like the whispering of the wind.

St. Michael's victory, someone says, pointing toward the church.

It stretches above me, and without surrounding structures, it seems to reach even higher into the sky than the others. My own insignificance tugs at my heart, and I stop in my tracks, studying the steeple and domed clock tower.

It is then that I see the statue—the shiny angel with its wings spread, the spear and cross above it. St. Michael, strong and fearless, threatens the lowly creature beneath his foot.

There are other statues, positioned around St. Michael, but they lack the luster of the angel, the victory and the mission. They look on without acting, waiting to be delivered from the enemy but not willing to conquer themselves.

The image burns in my mind.

Returning to the emigrant barracks, I cannot seem to forget the statue of St. Michael in all his glory, ready at any moment to destroy the darkness beneath him. He was not frightened or fearful, but ready.

Am I ready?

The boardinghouse near the port is crowded, far too many emigrants crammed inside of it. By the looks of it, many go to America for the same reason I do—they are tired of the hardship and want something better. But there are others that go to escape religious persecutions, like the Jews, and there are still others that go in search of adventure.

I wash my face. The cold water sends shivers down my face and neck. I am not used to mirrors. Mania owned a small one but forbade me from ever holding it. The only glimpses of my reflection have come from the church mirror or at Amalia's entry.

I try not to study myself too long, but my reflection is unrecognizable to me. It is strange to have lived in a body for so long without knowing the other side, the side that everyone else must see. I comb my fingers through my hair, and I cannot help but think of Marja's words. *I've never seen hair quite your color—the mixture of reds, browns, and even some blonde; it's lovely with your dark eyes.*

I pull the waves to the back of my head and fasten it into a braid. I have already spent too much time in this room, too much time looking at my reflection, but I glance once more.

Am I ready? The question still comes without an answer.

I only know I was ready to leave my life in Durliosy behind, but that is so very different from being prepared for what lies ahead.

Twelve

Jaką miarką mierzysz, taką ci odmierzą.
What goes around comes around.

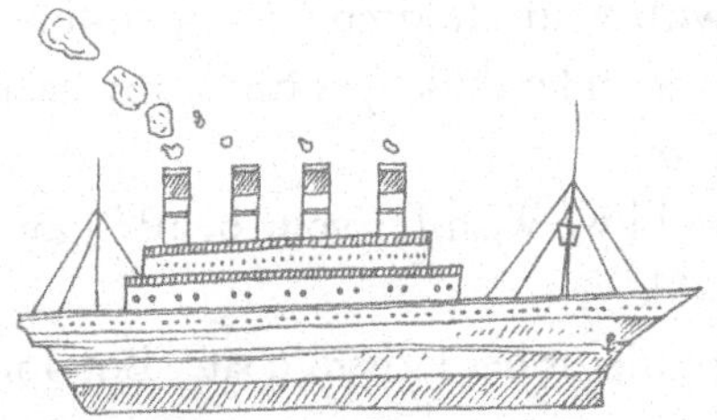

Marja's words haven't left me. *Look for someone you can trust, and stay by them.* I've watched a Polish family for the last three days. There is safety in the father's watch, kindness in the mother's touch. That alone leads me to believe I can trust them.

But I board the ship tomorrow, and I'm running out of time.

The passenger hall is quiet, and I stand behind the Polish family in a single-file line, waiting for my final examination. My initial bathing, physical examination, and vaccinations happened upon arriving at the barracks, but my belongings were searched and disinfected only yesterday.

I tap the mother on the shoulder, and blood rushes to my cheeks. "Pardon me," I say. I hesitate, watching as the man behind her glares back at me.

She startles, but smiles. "Yes?"

The father's shoulders stiffen, and he crosses his arms in front of him. His eyes narrow. "Beata," he says in warning.

But his wife steps closer. She smiles, and small lines around her light eyes appear. "Can I help you, Miss?"

The softness of her voice calms me. "My name is Stefania. I am traveling alone," I say.

Their young daughter peers around her mother and smiles. The gap between her teeth reminds me of Bronia, and I smile back.

The father's brows knit together, and his bottom lip juts to the side. "We see that. What of it?"

His wife cranes her head toward him. "Igor, she is young. Let her speak."

Igor sighs, and his shoulders relax. He nods at me, urging me to continue.

"I can help with your children," I say, smiling at the little girl and her older brother. Her dark eyes tug at my heart, reminding me of Bronia even more.

"And why would we wish for your help?" Igor asks, pulling his wife closer to his side.

The daughter pulls at her father's coat. "But Tatuś, why can't we play with her?"

He grunts. "Julita, she is a stranger."

I stammer forward, almost losing my balance. "But I am used to caring for my nephews, my niece. I only need someone to travel with."

"You mean as a protection for you?" he asks, scanning me again.

I swallow. "And as a help to you."

He grunts, waving a large hand at me and jerking his head to the side.

"Of course you will travel with us," Beata says, a warm smile spreading across her delicate features.

"Beata?" Igor asks, his mouth gaping open.

She nods at him. "Yes, I could use some help, Igor." She places both hands on her growing belly. "This girl is young and alone. I do not think she will bring any trouble."

I nod, biting my lip. "None at all, sir."

Igor inhales, his large nostrils flaring. He lowers his voice, directing it at his wife. "I will not be responsible for whatever trouble comes of this."

"Certainly not," Beata says. She holds her hand out to me. "Stefania, we would be happy to have you travel with us."

I sigh, relief washing over me. "Thank you."

Julita giggles. "Will she sleep by us, on the boat, Matka?"

"Of course, if she would like."

"She will hear Tatuś snore!" Julita says, letting out a shriek of laughter.

Beata casts a look of reprimand, but continues. "Steerage tickets provide scarcely. We will ride as cargo and only have wood bunks to sleep in, but it shouldn't be for more than two weeks."

Igor grasps her hand, pulling her forward in the line. "But first, we must finish our examinations."

Beata waves her hand. "Yes, we'll see you on the tender, Stefania."

The Hamburg America Steamship Company. The SS Acilia. Sailing every week from Hamburg.

I study my ticket. All the symbols are meaningless to me. I cannot read it, but I remember what Oliwjer told me it said, and despite the cryptic scratches on the white paper, I know that tomorrow these symbols will mean everything to me. It is my path forward. I will be one step closer tomorrow.

"Next," a worker yells, ushering me to an examination room.

The surgeons already examined me upon my arrival to the barracks, and every morning and evening since. America will not allow the diseased to enter. Now, the police make their own examination.

"Papers," the man at the desk says, his mustache twitching as he speaks. Golden-rimmed spectacles balance on the brim of his nose. He leans over a large ledger, ink staining the edges of his fingers.

I hand him my papers, passport, ticket, and examination results.

"Name?" he asks.

"Stefania Marzewska."

He dips his pen, scratching it along the ledger. "Age? Schooling? Can you read or write?"

"Sixteen," I say swallowing. I shake my head. "Very little schooling, and no, I cannot read or write."

"Do you have family you will be joining in America? Are you travelling alone?" he asks.

"I join my brother Wiktor in Baltimore, and I travel with another Polish family," I say. It is a relief I found the courage to approach Beata and Igor.

More scratches on the paper.

"Your mental state? Have you ever been institutionalized?" he asks without looking up.

"No."

"Have you ever worked as a prostitute?" He pauses, glancing up.

Heat floods my face. I shake my head and swallow the lump forming in my throat. "Never," I say, but it comes out as a whisper.

He pushes the spectacles higher on his nose. "And what about the law? Have you ever been detained or questioned for criminal behavior?"

I cringe. "No."

"How much money do you have?" the man asks, still setting his pen to the ledger.

I show him my thirty dollars.

He sets the pen down and smiles. "Looks like you're on your way to America. Follow this hall to the double doors. There you can board a boat. You'll stay there until you board the ship tomorrow." He stamps my ticket and papers, handing them back.

I hope the journey will pass like the dream I feel it is, this cloudy sequence of events where I am continually reminded of my dependence on others.

Thirteen

Z próżnego i Salomon nie naleje.
From nothing, nothing will be.

Like cattle to a pen, we are herded onto the boat. The steerage deck fills to capacity, and yet still more come.

Beata leans against a railing, her other hand grasping at her back in pain. She is only midway through her pregnancy, but she is not faring well. She does not complain, but neither can she hide her discomfort.

"Someday, I will own my own hotel in America," Wojciech, the son, says proudly. "Then I will stay in suites and ride in important carriages."

I smile at him. If only I could get to America to start over, that would be enough for me.

"Wojciech, America brings many promises," Igor says. His deep voice shakes, and worry stretches across his downcast lips. "It will be better, but you must not forget, a Pole will always be a Pole. America does not forget, and we will never forget either."

I hope I will forget.

Julita giggles. "I am going to be an American," she says between her crooked teeth. She wraps her arms around her father's leg.

Igor's shoulders fall, and he looks off into the distance. Perhaps he will save his words for a later day.

A day of hope for so many—there is laughter and excitement, talk of better days and freedom from starvation. Many words are spoken, and most in languages I do not understand, but hope rings clear in each of them. America does hold promises, like Beata's husband said.

I only hope that they are true.

Cheers resonate across the deck, and the ship leaves the harbor. It glides across the water, slowly at first, but once distanced from the port, it picks up speed, slicing through the water.

I sit in silence, watching the water sparkle, the waves trailing the boat hind. The rhythmic sway rocks me as a mother might.

"Stefania," Igor says. "Why are you traveling alone?"

I turn, surprised. I untie my scarf, raising it to the crown of my head. "It is hard to explain to someone like you, someone with a family."

He squints, placing a strong hand on his hip. "You did not leave family?"

I hesitate. How much to tell, I cannot decide. I exhale, licking my dried lips. "I leave my brother's family, yes, but I go to another brother. Wiktor is in America. He sent my passage. My parents died years ago, and I have not belonged in Durliosy since. I cannot stay where I do not belong."

Igor nods, still looking out to the ocean. "And is that all? I get the feeling you are hiding something."

I am, but nothing that I am ashamed of—only things I wish forgotten. "Nothing that will cause you trouble," I say.

"Are you certain?" he asks. There is strength in his stance, power in his gaze. What would it be like to have him as a father, a protector?

"I will not stay by your family if you do not want me to, but I am glad to tend the children when Beata needs help."

He shifts his weight, lifting a hand to scratch his chin. The wrinkles near his eyes grow. "My wife is with child, and it makes her ill. The ship will only make it worse. I know she could use your help. In return, I will act as your guardian until I see you safely to your brother."

"Thank you," I say.

He grunts. "You must be careful. There are eyes everywhere."

Eyes everywhere. I look around the boat. No one seems to be aware of me.

Darker and more dreadful than I could have imagined, the ship's smell is enough to make one sick—the odor of vomit, waste, and sweat follow me wherever I go. But the motion of the ship on the water, like a carriage ride that never ends, only makes it worse. The storms jolt the ship so severely, seizing control of everyone and everything.

I have never been more powerless.

The saltwater in the washrooms stings my skin and eyes, so I have given up on washing myself, as most have. The stench has become inescapable. It feels as if the hundreds of us have been sent here to die.

Some have died. Just yesterday, they buried three bodies at sea.

They buried one more this morning—a child. The parents watched with tears streaming down their faces. The mother lunged after her child, but the father held her back, anger in his voice.

I am not sure if he was angry at the crew for the sickening conditions, his wife for trying to follow the child, or God for allowing the child to die.

It is heartbreaking. To be so close, yet lose so much.

Back and forth, up and down. Up and down, back and forth. The boat's constant rocking is nothing like those of a mother putting a child to sleep, as I first supposed. The ship's movements are jarring, at times disturbingly rough, and always disorienting.

I shut my eyes, pretending I am already there, already setting foot in America. I imagine a land far warmer and greener than Durliosy. There are no rocks, no oppression, no starvation. And most of all, there is less pain—less pain of losing my parents, enduring the servitude, and deserting my dearest friend and niece.

I imagine I am leaving all the pain forever, stepping into the sun for the first time.

My thoughts are interrupted by a soft tap on my shoulder. I turn, surprised to see a boy standing to my side. "Do you remember me from the train?" He asks, smiling widely. He winks. "The name is Petar."

Without his teasing friend, he does not seem so scary. My eyes narrow and I nod. "Yes. You were very bad on the train. You and your friend teased me."

Petar pushes a hand through his dark hair, rolling his head backward, laughing. He tucks his hands into his coat, and I can see that he is nervous. "Yes, we did tease you. We did not think we would see you again."

"So, you thought it more reason to torture me?" I ask, no hint of a smile.

Petar clears his throat, but still smiles. "Yes, but we had traveled far. It was refreshing to see a girl our own age."

I nod, forcing myself to be civil. "Is the other boy on the ship?"

Petar grins. "Yes. Would you like to see him?" He lifts his chin to the side, pointing with a shake of his head to a group huddled across the deck. His friend lifts a hand when he sees me, smiling widely.

My cheeks burn, and I look away. "No," I say.

Petar nods, looking down at his shoes and inching closer. "Do you think you will tell me your name at last? We still have some time, and I would not mind making another friend."

Our eyes meet, and I hesitate.

"Wojciech stole my scarf," Julita says, running to my side. Her breath is staggered, and she leans her head against my abdomen.

I pick her up. "Don't you worry. We will get it back, and perhaps some food? Hmm?"

"I am hungry," she says, wiping her tear-stained cheeks.

I step away from the railing but stop, turning back to Petar. Perhaps I could do with another friend along the way.

He lowers his head, retreating.

"Stefania," is all I say.

His eyes brighten, his smile returning. "It's nice to meet you, Stefania."

"Not go back?" he asks. Petar's eyes widen in disbelief.

I shake my head, not meeting his gaze. Petar would not understand. He carries on with such optimism, somehow sure of good things to come. "And you? Why go back, after all this?" I ask, motioning toward the boat.

"For my family," he says, shrugging. "My friend and I go to work in the coal mines in Pennsylvania. Men came to Opanci to recruit, and they offered more money than we could ever make there. We will work, then return to Croatia." He pauses, and his dark eyes flicker with the reflection of the stars. "And what will you do in America?"

"I am not sure, but my brother promises there is work. Maybe I will work in a factory," I say, unsure of what that work entails. "But I will find something, and when I do, I will work and save. I will eat well and sleep, knowing that there will be means for the next day."

He laughs at this. "More likely you will find a husband."

I scoff. I have not left Jozef and Andrzejek so that someone else can take care of me, take control.

Petar's smile falls, and he crosses his arms. "Stefania, you will have your chance to marry, and you will make a good wife. You do not think so?"

Words catch in my throat. "Maybe one day, Petar. But that is not why I come to America. I could have married in Poland if I really wanted to."

Petar nods, one side of his lip rising. "You are young. Maybe you will change your mind. Who knows what America will bring? Perhaps you will find your one person. No one is happy alone."

"Maybe one day," I say again, in hopes of changing the subject. The wind bites at my nose, and I push my chin into the collar of my coat, shivering. I wipe my hand across my face, and dirt and grime accumulate on my glove. I smile. "I hope America brings a good wash."

Petar laughs. "Yes. And clean clothes."

We sit for a moment more, watching the sun disappear on the horizon. The light dissipates so quickly; darkness creeps in rapidly and thick.

Petar points to a star in the early evening sky. "Do you think that is the star directing the ship?" he asks. He shakes his head and smiles. "I do not know if they use the stars as guides any more, but they did once. Do you think there is a star guiding each of us?" he asks more seriously.

I shrug. "It is a pretty thought."

Petar's friend calls to him, and he raises his brows. "Looks like I am needed. Goodnight, Stefania."

"Petar?" I call out, before he is out of hearing.

He stops, turning back to me.

"Do you think America will be everything we believe it will?"

This question hangs in the air, and the background conversation seems to disappear. I know there is too much emotion in my voice. I clear my throat, forcing myself to smile.

Petar reaches for me, touching my arm. "We cannot know for sure until we get there, but America is an opportunity—an opportunity to start over, to live a new life, maybe to not be hungry so much, or perhaps to find a new dream." He pauses, kicking his shoe against the wooden deck.

Our eyes meet, and I swallow a sob.

He shakes his head. "Do you think so many people would go if it was not worth it? Would they bury their children at sea, Stefania, if there was another way?"

"Another way for what?" I ask.

He stares down, in what looks like pity, his lips pressed and eyes wide. "Another way to survive, to go on. America is not just about opportunity. For some of us, it is the only way we can go on. We have to believe in it."

Tears prick my eyes. He put to words what my heart has been competing to communicate—the words I need to hear. I had to come. The future was too bleak, my life worth only the work I did. America became the only way out of what I was living. It, like the boat, kept me from drowning the last three months with Jozef and Mania. It is the hope of America that pulls me through my loss of Andrzejek and Bronia.

Petar must see the realization in my face. He does not say anything else; he does not need to. Instead, he touches my arm for a moment more and then disappears to the other side of the deck.

Fourteen

Do odważnych świat należy.
Fortune favors the bold.

I can see it—Baltimore. The inlet of water acts as a gate, ushering me into my new land, my new life. If it were possible, I would swim to the shore and dig my soles into the soil straight away.

Across the sea, there was a life of servitude. But here? I close my eyes, taking in the possibilities. The worst is past. Lightness has replaced the darkness.

"It is not over yet," Petar says, nudging me. "There will be more examinations like those in Hamburg."

I shake my head, smiling. "But we are here."

"It is a cause for celebration," Petar says, turning to his friend. "Shall we?"

They sing the only song in English they know, "For He's a Jolly Good Fellow."

Laughter comes, but so do tears, and I am not alone. There are many that shed tears—tears of joy, tears of relief, tears of hope.

I find Beata in her bunk, her dirt and sweat-stained face pressed against her bag. "Beata, we have almost made it. I saw Baltimore."

A flicker of understanding crosses her dark eyes, and she tries to smile.

I grab her hand. "Do you want to see it?"

She nods.

For once, the stairs are empty, the bunk room bare. The other passengers have already gone to the deck. They are eager, as I am, to see this part of the journey behind us.

The noise from above is deafening, and Beata's eyes dart around at the throngs overhead. I worry her nerves cannot take the excitement.

"Do you want to go back to the bunk?" I ask.

Her breathing is shallow, but she shakes her head. She pauses a moment, clinging to a post for support. "No, I need to see it."

We come by the deck, slower than most but equally as thrilled. I pull Beata through the crowd, heading toward Petar, knowing he will let her by the guardrail to see the city.

It is a fight to get there. People push and pull.

To my surprise, I feel the weight of Beata's arm against my shoulder less with each step. She grows stronger from the anticipation. Then she sees it and lets out a wail. She trembles. I hold her weight again, though this time it is not because of sickness, but of relief.

The ship comes to a stop along the port, the propellers halt, and the crewmen organize their efforts. Men shout in all different directions, yet they move in harmony. There are men directing the passengers, others adjusting the rails and ramps, and still more managing the ship.

I stand beside Beata and Petar, huddled mere inches apart.

Igor leans between his wife and me. "Stefania, we will pray for you," he says in a soft, broken manner. He reaches to Beata, and she falls into his embrace.

She keeps ahold of my hand, and she clasps it tighter, whispering in a weakened voice. "Thank you. The children, Igor, and I could not have made it without you. You are like family to us all."

Tears leak from my eyes, dripping down my cheeks. I swat at them with my scarf. For some reason this makes me laugh.

Igor joins me, and soon we are all huddled in an overcrowded hug. Julita is at my waist, Beata to one side, and Igor and Wojciech on the other.

Wojciech is the first to break away. "You all stink," he says, gasping for breath.

I laugh, my cheeks stinging from the exercise.

We stand together, admiring our new land.

My legs shake, but I walk down the ramp. It is as if I am still on the boat, and I cannot find my footing on land. Yet with each step, I see Baltimore a little clearer.

Workers direct us to the processing room in a brick building. We take a seat on the benches—row upon row of benches—and await more instructions.

English is not like Polish or German or Russian. I do not recognize the timbre or intonation. A man approaches Igor and motions for us to put our luggage beneath the benches. We follow suit, accepting a small piece of paper from the man—a number.

"We start the examinations now," a voice behind me whispers. Peter smiles. "You know, the medical examinations and questions. They decide if we can stay here, in America."

I smile back, though my insides twist in knots. I tuck my papers and money a little deeper into my coat pocket and set down my bag.

"It will be okay, Stefania," Petar says, brushing past me toward his friend. "We made it here alive, didn't we?"

I smile, watching as Petar disappears into a line of boys.

I do not think I will see him again.

Fifteen

Oko za oko, ząb za ząb.
You must meet roughness with roughness.

"Stella! Is it really you?" My brother wraps his arms around me, pulling me off the concrete steps.

He is taller than I remember, his arms stronger.

"Wiktor," I say, squeezing him back.

His dark hair hangs across his forehead, the waves and curls just as handsome as I remember them. He loosens his hold of me, grinning. "That was quite the ride, yes? I am sure you have more than a few stories you could tell me now."

I smile, shaking my head. "Yes, but I think there are better stories to be told than that of the stench and the dread of death."

He clicks his tongue, dropping back a step. "Your story isn't so different than mine or the thousands like you. It makes for good memories later, though maybe not so much now."

I nod, shuffling to the side to avoid a nearby carriage. My brother takes me through the streets of Fells Point, pointing out the best bakeries and places of work. He says this is where most of the Polish and other Eastern Europeans settle.

"Stella, you will soon learn to call the city home. People are people, no matter what language they speak. Of course, you'll have to learn some English. The American-born are nicer if you try to speak their language."

I say nothing, distracted with my new world. Polish will always be my language. Perhaps, there is a bit of my father's Polish pride left in me still.

"Are you hungry?" my brother asks.

"Yes, very. Thanks, Wiktor," I say, rubbing one hand against my stomach.

He grins. "Call me Vic, Stella. We are in America now. Wiktor is a part of the old country. So many strange names from all over, it's impossible to say any of them right."

I grip the leather strap of my bag tighter. "Then I will call you Vic."

He smiles again, revealing his large white teeth. I had almost forgotten the way his lips disappear when he smiles.

"Is it as easy to find work as they say?" I ask, scanning the crowd of immigrants like me, eager to start a new life.

Vic raises a brow. "It is easy if you do not care what kind of work. A girl like you can find a job in the sweatshops."

"The sweatshops?" I ask.

"Yes, there are many factories in Fells Point." He shrugs, and I notice how much stronger he has become. His arms are as thick as my legs and his neck is the size of a tree trunk.

The city air is thick, so thick I can see it, taste it. If I were to reach my hand out, I am sure I would feel the texture of it. My steps slow and I catch my breath, wondering how those around me carry on so unaffected by the pollution.

"It's the factories, you know," Vic says, putting his arm around my shoulder. "You get used to it after a while. Eventually you will forget what real air smells like."

He pulls me to a bench near an alley. We sit and he pulls out a sandwich from his pocket, handing it to me. I eat slowly at first, aware how closely he is watching me. The bread is so much better, softer, than anything we had on the ship, and the meat is sweet and fresh.

Vic still stares at me like I am a stranger. Maybe he is as surprised by my appearance as I am by his. His face is wider, his shoulders stronger. He has changed so much in four years, and yet he is still the same. How is that possible? My brother Vic is now a man.

After I finish eating, we weave in and out of the city's grid once more, and somehow everything starts to feel more familiar. It's as if Poland herself boarded the ship alongside of me, relocating to this street. The smells, the sights, the people—it reminds me of where I came from.

Yet it is different—new and hopeful.

Vic takes me to a corner building, across from a large factory.

"My favorite place," he says, waving at a man. "I told you I would come, and even better, you can meet my sister."

"Stella, is it?" the man asks. He is only trying to be polite.

I nod.

He turns to the side, gasping for breath, apparently appalled by my stench.

I instinctively move a bit further from him, and my cheeks burn in humiliation.

"Just arrived here then?" he asks Vic.

"Yeah, she still needs a good bath," my brother says, nudging me with his elbow. Vic jerks his head upward, his chin a mode of pointing. "Stella, I have to take care of something. Can you wait here? It will only take a moment."

They start for the brick building and my eyes trail them. Boisterous sounds emanate from it, the shouts and jeering of men so loud that they overpower the horseshoes' clicks against the streets and the bells of the bicycles. "Are you going in there?" I ask, trying not to sound as alarmed as I feel.

"Your brother has an account to settle. It should not take long," the man by my brother explains. "Turnbol House. It is where the men gather to play cards and drink. That is also where they hold the boxing matches." He stops, crossing his arms. "Not a place for a girl."

"Wait here," Vic says, walking away with his friend.

I lean against the brick façade, staring down at my skirt. The brown fabric has darkened to near-black, dirt encrusted along the hem. I do need a bath.

Just then the double doors burst open and two bodies tumble through the doorway, the figures becoming a blur of splattering blood and flinging fists. One of the men is taller and towers over his opponent. He gives a final blow, effectively sending the smaller man down to the ground. The winner stares down at the defeated man, his face red from the exertion and a trickle of blood sliding down his left cheek.

"Then you were right, Marco," a voice from inside the house calls. "Your brother is worth betting on, even against Tony."

I hear men laugh in response, but I cannot look away from the man on the ground. He struggles to stand, falling back to his side.

I gasp, rushing to his side. I feel the man's pulse, run my fingers over his bruised eye. "Are you alright?" I ask.

The man standing over the wounded one startles when he hears me. He meets my eye and takes a step back, wiping his bruised hands through dark hair. "This is no place for a girl," he says, lifting his chin. His brown eyes narrow, and the hint of a smile spreads across his cheeks.

The men beyond the door laugh once more, their attention now fixed on me.

In an instant, my face reddens, burning in anger and embarrassment. I grit my teeth and stand, backing away from the defeated boxer.

"Yes, go back to your mother, girl," the dark-haired man says, effectively stopping me in my tracks.

My shoulders tremble, and for a moment, I contemplate throwing my own punch at the arrogant man. The thought startles me—it is so unlike me, and I cannot understand how the boxing man has affected me so dramatically.

"Stella," my brother calls, his hurried footsteps along the grass getting louder. He grasps my arm and pulls me toward the road, seemingly oblivious to the spectacle before me. "Sorry it took so long. You know how it is."

I nod, aware of the man's presence behind me still. "I am ready to leave. I do not like the smell of this part of town."

Vic laughs, shaking a finger at me. The lines around his mouth and chin deepen, his dimples accentuating his large smile. "Ah, yes—the gaming house, not at all the place for you, though I'd argue you stink worse."

I match my brother's footsteps, refusing to glance behind myself again. I can do without seeing that man again.

I finally ask what I have been wondering since I arrived. "Where is Stanislaus?"

"Stan." Vic grunts, turning his face away. "Everyone calls him Stan now. I don't know where he is. The truth is, we had a falling out of sorts last year. He left, and I haven't heard from him since. But a few guys said he went to the mines in Pennsylvania."

"What kind of falling out?" I ask. I have not seen my brother Stan since I was twelve years old. He is older than Vic, and we were never close.

Vic shrugs. "Oh, it was more than just one thing." He pulls out a cigarette and puts it between his teeth, striking a match against the pavement.

"What happened?"

He takes a few puffs and turns to me. "Money, I suppose. I always hoped he would come back, but he never has. And now you are here." His voice trails off, and I can tell his mind has taken him back to Poland. "How are Jozef and Franz and Amalia?"

I shrug, biting the inside of my cheek. "Amalia is happy. Her children are sweet, and I will miss them. And then, Franz—when I left, Franz chased me down the street, telling me that I was dishonest, that I should not run away from Jozef and God."

Vic lets out an exasperated sigh, half shaking as he laughs. "Franz has turned into a man of the cloth, I see. But don't you worry, Stella. You were right in not telling Jozef. I can't see how he or Mania would ever let you out of their home. They used you for labor."

I squint, staring off in the distance. There is so much more I could say, but I cannot find the words without feeling the emotions of it all. Instead, I just nod. "Sometimes, I wish that leaving Poland for a new life could mean that I also leave my past. And everyone in it."

Vic turns to me, and his lips curl into a sad smile, the usual lightness in his voice gone. "The old country—that's what everyone calls the place they came from. Most don't talk about it. You can leave it behind too. We won't talk about it anymore," he pauses, waiting for a response, then adds, "unless you wish."

My eyes gloss over and I feel a burning in my chest. "Yes, let's leave it at that—the old country."

Vic stops, pointing at a factory. The building reaches a few floors high, a humming emitting from the windows. "Let's see if we can get you a job, yeah?"

"What is this place?" I ask, staring at the men unloading boxes and hauling them into the building.

"A factory—sewing." Vic points to a girl about my age that exits the front gate. "Most of the girls like you work here. It makes for long days, but the factory will pay the bills and provide room and lodging."

Sewing all day sounds much easier than hauling a cart to market. I smile. "Yes, let's see about the job."

Vic leads me through the front door.

My eyes dart from one thing to the next—the large room before me, the piles of neatly folded clothing, the boxes, and the men hauling goods in and out of the building. The hum from above is piercing, like a hive of wasps constantly buzzing in my ears.

A short, stout man approaches me. "Job inquiries are to be made in the upstairs office." He points to a staircase across the room. Then he turns to my brother. "I don't think you'll have much luck, but your friend might."

Vic grins. "My sister."

The man nods, returning to his work in the inventory.

With each stair, the humming grows in volume. The wooden staircase leads to a large room, full of women. There are about twenty different groupings, separated only by the brick pillars and wandering supervisors. The bare windows and unfinished floor serve as the only soundboard for the constant noise of the machines, the overhanging pipes and lights the only distraction from the busy floor. Piles of clothing lay next to each woman—some looking no older than children—and the supervisors weave in and out of their groups, their watchful eyes lingering on the slightest hint of idleness.

Vic touches my arm. "Stella, this way," he says, pointing toward a doorway to my right.

We enter, and my brother begins talking to the man at the desk in English. They talk for a few minutes, and I can't understand anything other than their sideway glances and my brother's gestures.

The man waves for me to follow him, leaving Vic beside the desk. He takes me to talk to a Polish woman named Aniela, a maternal-looking figure with a pointed nose.

"We start you at nine dollars a week with room and lodging, which is better than what you'll find elsewhere—that's for sure," the woman says, cranking her neck to the side. Her blonde hair is tied in a bun on the top of her head. "Your brother says you sew?"

My head bobs up and down. "Yes, well, mending. I have not used a machine like those here—"

The woman puts her hand up, silencing me. "You will learn. Take this sheet of paper with you to your supervisor—I'll point him out later—and he'll give you your rooming assignment. Now, your work is crucial. You arrive every morning by seven. Each day you will be given a pile of work. You finish your work, you go home. You stay until it is completed, you understand?"

I nod again. "I understand."

"Now, I have to say it, Miss—?" She stops, staring at me in question.

"Marzewska."

"Miss Marzewska, then." She smiles, and I notice she is missing a few teeth. "They tell me I have to say it to everyone. The truth is, we have more than enough women to choose from. You came just as we released another young woman for incompetency. Work hard, Miss Marzewska, and you will keep the job." She pauses until I nod again, smiling. "And welcome to America."

Sixteen

Jak sobie pościelesz, tak się wyśpisz.
What you reap is what you sow.

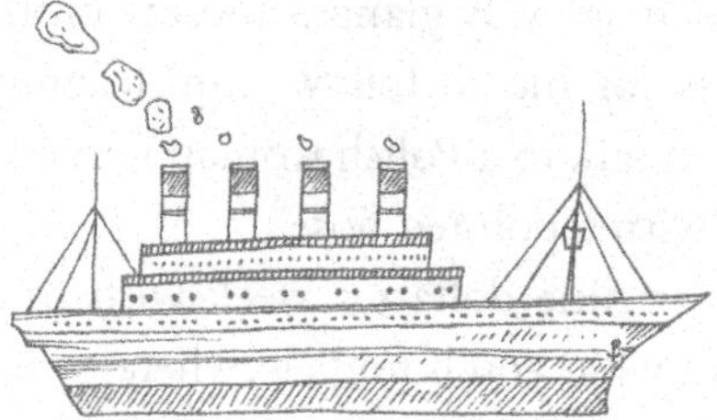

"Charlie, do me a favor and lock the doors to the staircase, won't you?" one of the supervisors says, scribbling some words down on his notepad. "The women are taking too many breaks. We can't afford them leaving."

I inwardly cringe, making sure to keep my head down. It is not that I mind missing the breaks. I would rather work through my pile without one. It is just that locking the doors feels forceful, wrong. It's dehumanizing.

The factory work is long and monotonous, but not difficult. The machines are faster than sewing by hand, and the labor is less strenuous on my back and legs than the work on the farm, even with the constant pedaling of my feet.

The only drawback is the needle. Sometimes I forget how quickly it comes down, and more than once I have had it go through my finger completely. A quick salve is enough to stop the bleeding and it heals fine, even if it takes a while. I have heard tales of girls that have had to lose a finger because of the injury. I count myself lucky that my needle wounds are only in the tip of my fingers.

My roommate, Tia, tells me it gets easier. She says that the machine soon becomes like another arm and that I will become so aware of the needle and the hum that I will not have to think about it.

I hope she is right.

Potica. I lick my lips, glancing at the sweet bread behind the counter.

Every Saturday afternoon, Vic takes me to the café. The aroma of breads and sausage, pierogies, bigos, and meats can be smelled far before we open the shop door. Each time, I tell myself I will choose something other than the sweet-filled bread, but when I go to the counter, my mouth waters at the sight of it. Walnuts and cinnamon—it's just how Amalia made it, only better.

"Potica again?" The woman behind the counter asks, grinning widely.

I hand her my coins. "Yes, and coffee."

She winks and turns to Vic.

It is a busy café with about ten tables, but already there are people lined up out the door. This place is part of the Polish district, as Vic calls it, so everyone seems to speak it, or at least understand it. I recognize a few German and Russian words, as well as several other Slavic dialects from the old country.

We sit at two of the last open seats.

"Vic," a light-haired girl from a nearby table says, waving. She stands, apparently finished with her meal. Her eyes dart from my brother to me, a question in her gaze. "How have you been?"

Vic looks caught off guard, but he smiles, his dimple deepening. "Alice, it's been too long since I saw you out dancing. Have you met my sister?" He motions to me. "Stella, this is my friend Alice."

I glance at the pretty girl beside me—light hair and blue eyes, thick black eyelashes. She blushes. "Vic, it's so nice you have a sister to keep you company. I have often thought it sad that you were alone, especially after Stan left. Are you working at the docks still?"

Vic shakes his head. "Nah, I thought about shucking oysters, but I decided to go to the meat packing plant instead. They don't give me a job every day, but I go early and wait at the gate, hoping the man will tap me on the shoulder for a day's work." His lips curl into a smile and he leans toward Alice. "I think he likes my work; he taps my shoulder most days I go."

Alice twists her fingers around her braids. "But it pays well, Vic? You are getting along?"

Vic laughs. "No, it pays worse than almost anything, but I survive. I have other ways of getting money."

I meet his eyes, waiting for an explanation. But he looks away.

"Do you go dancing still?" Alice asks, biting the edge of her bottom lip.

"It is nice to get out, and now that my sister is here, yes. I have to go to keep the filth from her." He nudges me, winking.

Alice sways from side to side, hesitating at the door. "Then maybe I'll see you."

My brother lifts a brow, nodding. His shoulders hunch forward and he pushes his hands deeper into his trousers. "If you'll save me a dance?"

"Yeah, I think I can manage that," she says, blushing and leaving the café with a grin so large it reaches her eyes.

A café worker brings my bag of my sweet bread, a plate of pierogi and sausage to my brother. My mouth waters at the smell.

I bite my lip, flicking my head in the direction of Alice. "How long have you known that girl? She is pretty, Vic."

Vic only stares at me. "The waitress? I've never seen her before."

My brows rise, and I tilt my head, nudging him with my elbow. "No, Vic. Alice."

His face turns a shade of pink, and he shakes his head. "Not a word, Stella."

I take a bite of my bread, staring down to keep from laughing. It seems he has become a man in more ways than one. He never used to blush at girls.

"Vic," someone else calls.

I am not good with strangers, and it seems my brother knows everyone in Fells Point. Two men nod at Vic, the shorter one waving. I lean back against my chair, a familiar feeling creeping into my stomach.

"Are you keeping all the ladies company again?" the shorter man asks in a mixture of Polish and Croatian. He places his hands on

Vic's shoulders and smirks. "I saw you talking to Alice. Still sweet on her?"

Vic laughs, holding out his hand. "Nah."

"I guess I shouldn't ask such a thing while you're entertaining another girl," my brother's friend says, smiling.

Vic almost chokes on his bite of pierogi, shaking his head. "Nah, Marco. Mike, have you met my kid sister?" He touches my arm. "This is Stella. And Stella, meet Marco and Mike Nosic, brothers."

Marco inches toward me, smiling widely. "You never said you had your sister here."

Vic shrugs. "I have to keep her from the likes of men like you."

There is a gleam in Marco's light eyes, and he punches my brother's shoulder. "I can see why."

I glance behind Marco, assessing the older and taller brother behind him. Mike does not smile, but he returns my gaze. His eyes are dark, almost black even, contrasting with his light brown hair. There is a scab along his temple, a yellowing bruise beneath it.

My brother takes another bite, not bothering to swallow it before speaking. "I am taking Stella dancing tonight again, near the old shipbuilding yard. You guys should come—I could do with a few guys to talk to."

Marco puts his arm around his brother, laughing. "We'd probably rather talk to the girls than you, Vic." He winks at me. "You like to go dancing, Stella?"

My stomach knots. I still haven't learned to talk to boys. I nod. "Yes, it is what makes the work bearable."

The older brother chuckles at my response, and I feel my face grow hotter.

"Well, maybe we'll go, if only so I can have a dance with your sister, Vic," Marco says.

At this, Vic clears his throat and points to the brothers. "I forgot to tell you, Stella, where these guys work. They work in the loading docks, like many. It makes them strong and helps them find other ways to make ends meet."

Marco's smile widens, but his brother Mike scowls.

I hesitate a moment, finally asking, "And what does that mean?"

Vic slapping his fists together. "They are both boxers, fighters of sorts. Best we've had at Turnbol's for a while now too—the Nosic brothers. I've only lost my betting money a few times on the pair." Vic smiles at Mike, throwing pretend jabs at his stomach.

Marco nods proudly. "And it'll only get better, Vic. Mike beat the Italian again—what was his name?" He lifts a finger. "Tony."

Boxers? My mouth is suddenly dry, remembering my first walk in Fells Point and the uncomfortable exchange with the boxing man. I glance once more at Mike, studying his bruised cheek and scabbed temple.

Mike looks back at me, my realization seeming to flicker back across his dark eyes and dry smile. He nods.

"So, Stella," Marco prods. "Do you think you'd give me a dance tonight?"

In my mind's eye, I envision Franz, standing at his pulpit, preaching of the carnalities that have swept the earth—gambling, fighting. My jaw tightens, my fists clenching. How did I not recognize Mike as the arrogant man from the gaming house that day?

"And you did not recognize my attempt to sidestep your impending offer," Vic teases. "Stella is barely older than a child. She doesn't want to dance with you—you and your brother are too old for her."

I try not to cringe at the word *child.*

Mike lifts a brow, clearly amused. He saw it—my disgust at being spoken of in such a patronizing manner.

My eyes dart downward, unable to hold his gaze.

"We will let her make her own choice, yeah, Vic?" Marco asks.

Vic rubs his hands together, wiping his mouth with a napkin. He doesn't answer Marco's questions about dancing. Instead, he nods and asks, "Will I see you later at Turnbol's?"

Marco slaps his hands together. "Of course."

My roommate, Tia, pushes me into the center, giggling as she does so. "Go, Stella, don't be afraid."

The old warehouse has been turned into a dance hall, as it is every Saturday night. Chairs line the outer walls, and a few musicians are gathered in a clump near the far end.

I shake my head, straightening my dress. "Ah, Tia," I say, clicking my tongue at her. I am starting to feel alive for once. I am starting to remember the Poland I left as a dark dream—a dream that is passing.

Her dark hair is twisted at the side into a low bun, and her light eyes glow green against her olive complexion. "Come on, I must show you how to do this dance."

She pulls at my hands, weaving in and out of couples. We get to the middle of the dancers, and Tia twirls me to the beat, skipping along to the rhythm. I can't help but laugh, watching as she loses herself in the music.

She stops, glaring at me, dropping my hands. "Stella, you aren't doing it. You have to feel the music. Come on."

I smile, tilting my head. "Maybe it would be different if I had a male partner. We are the only two girls dancing together. My brother already called me a child today, and this makes me feel more like one."

Tia's eyes light up, and she grabs my hands once more. "You're right. Maybe I just need to find you the right partner then."

I glance around. "Where's Vic?"

"Ah, Vic started dancing with Alice. And besides, I know a better partner for you."

For some reason, I let Tia lead me toward a group of boys. I laugh trying to keep up with her tugs on my hand. "Tia," I say between gasps, "you're going to make me fall."

She glances back at me and grins, sending me into the man in front of me. He turns at the impact, catching me at the wrists. His gaze meets mine, and the edge of his lips curl into a smile.

Suddenly my own smile vanishes and my mouth hangs open. "You," I say, gasping for breath. I pull away.

"So, you do remember me then?" Mike asks, his dark eyes glistening in the dim light.

He is only a foot away, and I realize just how tall he is. I turn back to find Tia, who has already secured herself a dancing partner.

"Not so fast," Mike says, stopping me in my tracks as he did that first day. "That day I first saw you, I didn't know you were Vic's sister."

My heart races, remembering his words. *No place for a girl. Go back to your mother.* The back of my neck burns hot, anger bubbling up my throat. "And if you had known, then you would have been less awful and disgusting?"

Mike's mouth twists into a smirk, ironically accentuating a newly formed scab along his jawline. "Disgusting? That's a bit harsh. I'm sure people box in Poland too. It might not be fit for a girl's eyes, but it isn't so bad."

My eyes widen. "It is not fit for anyone. It is barbaric."

His smile returns, this time his jaw jutting forward. There is a challenge in his expression. "It's not so different from what you do."

"Hardly," I say, wrapping my arms around my stomach. I cannot understand why I am so bold around Mike, so unafraid of speaking my mind. It is not like me.

"Oh, no? We are both fighting to survive, throwing our own punches and trying to dodge the swings life throws at us," he says. I cannot help but notice the way he shifts his weight from one side to the other, his hand raking through his thick hair.

But boxing and my work are *very* different, and comparing the two only infuriates me more. So, I turn from him again, hoping he will leave me alone.

"Wait 'til you've been here a while. Then you'll see. We aren't so different," Mike says, laughing, "except for you're a girl."

I swing back, lifting a finger toward him and meeting his eyes once more. "We are nothing like each other, and I am not a child."

Mike's smile disappears, his gaze falling to my outstretched hand. "What did you do to your finger?"

I look down at my sore finger, irritated that Mike noticed it. "It's nothing, just a needle through it."

Mike's brows arch in concern. "Did it hurt?"

I shake my head. "It happened so quickly that I hardly felt it, at least not until it was over." I take a step back, dropping my hands behind my back. "And besides, I thought you were a boxer. Why would you care if it hurt?"

Mike shakes his head, then cranks his neck to the side. His brown eyes seem to ignite, a reflective glow shining back at me. "You're right, I forgot. Boxers don't feel pain, but I would have thought you did. Most young girls do."

My mouth falls open, and in an instant, I find another new emotion—a mixture of instant anger, vulnerability, and defensiveness. My stubbornness takes root, a strange urge to combat his words and put him in my place.

"Well, are you going to dance with me or not?" Mike asks, extending his arms toward me.

My hands fly to my hips, and I puff, shaking my head. "You think I would dance with you after you insult me?"

He shrugs, wiping his hand across the stubble along his cheek. "Well, are you, or aren't you?"

I lift my chin even higher, sticking my nose up at him. "No, thank you."

The music picks up, a new song beginning, and I scan the dancers, searching for Tia. I can see her dancing with Vic, both enjoying it too much to notice my distress. My eyes flicker back to Mike.

He grins, and I notice the freckle on the right side of his face, just above his lip. His shoulders roll backward, and he steps to the side of me. "No matter, then."

He only takes a few steps before asking someone else to dance. The girl takes his arm eagerly, giggling as the pair of them take the center of the room. My stomach tightens and my face flushes. I cannot tell if I am more angry or humiliated—more upset at being forced to speak to him or being abandoned in the middle of the floor.

My hands ball into fists and my eyes disobediently follow Mike around the room.

The girl in his arms smiles, laughing at everything Mike has to say. Her hand grips his muscular shoulder each time they spin, and

Mike even brushes his hand against her cheek to wipe a strand of hair behind her ear.

My chest is on fire and my legs are like iron, anchored to the floor. Twisting my fingers around my skirt, I command myself to look away, not to give a thought to the miserable man. But then my eyes find him again, tracing his strong and tall outline in the faint light.

When the song ends, Mike twirls his partner once more, flashing his handsome smile at her. Then the woman leaves his side and Mike angles his head toward mine, locking eyes with me. A hint of mockery flares behind his expression, but there is something else. His eyes hold a secret, and they move across my features with such deliberate teasing, such unabashed attraction, that I find myself blushing.

I step behind a couple, intent on ignoring Mike, or at the very least not allowing him to see the effect of such a gaze. The blood rushes to my cheeks and my neck burns as hot as the fire in my chest.

"Stella, why aren't you dancing?"

My brother's voice startles me, and I gasp, swallowing quickly. I glance at Mike once more.

"Are you alright?" he asks, following my line of sight to Mike.

I shut my eyes, nodding. "Yes, yes, I am fine. It's just that I am not in the mood for dancing tonight."

Vic puts his arm around my shoulder, resting his chin on my head. "Let's get out of here then. Let's 'beat it,' as they say in English."

I smile, wrapping one arm around my brother's waist. "But only after you dance with me? It's been too many years since we last did."

Vic laughs. "Okay, but just one. I don't have enough charm to distract you from my dancing."

Seventeen

Cudze wady rychlej niż swoje obaczamy.
Somebody else's faults and misdeeds are
so much easier to spot than our own.

I am climbing the loft again, the ladder shaking against the wooden platform just as I remember it. My hand slips on a rung, a sliver sliding through it. I moan, clutching it to my chest.

"Ciocia Stella, is that you?"

I smile, forgetting the pain of my finger. "Bronia-sweet, yes."

I climb faster, but it's as if the ladder only lengthens, the top rung growing farther and farther away.

Bronia leans her head over the ledge, and her big brown eyes are filled with tears. The drops fall, pelting me on the forehead. "Why have you gone? Why did you leave me?"

My chest tightens, a lump forming at my throat. I shake my head, my own tears forming. "I had to."

Bronia only stares back at me, a question in her eyes. Then she pushes the ladder away, and I feel the legs of it teeter back and forth. It begins to fall backward. I fall further and further from the loft, effectively putting Bronia beyond reach. Then there is a loud thud. . .

I awake to my own cry, tears streaming down my cheeks. My pillow and hair are sopping wet. Even as I blink in the pale light, I can still see Bronia above me—her disheveled braids, her perfect little lips formed in a frown, and her small, outstretched hands that seem to be reaching and yet simultaneously pushing me away.

Sometimes I wonder if the ache will ever go away. I had to come to America, and yet it meant leaving a large part of my heart behind. The aching in my chest is as real and painful as the throbbing in my finger. I only hope that, like my finger, my heart will eventually heal.

I dress for work, putting on my dark skirt and cream blouse, all the while remembering Bronia. I brush my hair and twist it into a low bun. I try to push away the memories of brushing Bronia's tangled hair, the way she whined as I carefully sorted out the knots. I smile. A few fresh tears come. I cannot seem to shake the images, the sounds, the heartache. They flood into my mind.

At last I am presentable, but I fear the emotions of the morning will be visible for all to see. So, I walk alone, leaving before Tia has dressed.

The street is nearly empty, the sun not yet risen. A few girls walk ahead of me, but their footprints in the fallen snow are some of the first. I bury my chin in the collar of my coat, blowing warm breaths against the fabric. The factory is only two blocks from our boarding house, but in the cold, the distance seems much longer and farther.

"Stella?"

I turn at the sound of my name, my chin still tucked into the top of my coat.

Mike Nosic stands a few steps behind. His brown hair is hidden by a cap, except for the strands that lay against his forehead and around his ears. His hands are buried in his coat, his cheeks and the end of his nose pink from the chill. He nods when I turn, and his hurried footsteps halt as he reaches my side.

For a moment, I forget the freezing wind against my cheeks and the sadness of the morning. Instead, the muscles around my neck tighten, my lips forming into a scowl. My heart picks up speed, as if it is trying to carry me far away from the man beside me.

"You left the dance early. Marco says it is my fault," he says, his words creating a small cloud of mist in the coldness.

I lick my cracked lips. "Yes, well, I wasn't in the mood for dancing anyway."

Mike nods, pulling his collar around his neck. "So, it was me, then."

I shake my head, shrugging.

The warmth of his gaze surprises me. He smiles. "Well, I thought you could use these," he says, pulling his hand from his pocket and holding something in front of me.

He places a pair of leather finger guards, the kind with steel tips, into my hands.

My finger. I glance down at it, swollen and red. The throbbing seems to dissipate for a moment. "What's this for?"

Mike laughs, taking a step back. "For your fingers, of course. You've got to take better care of them if you want to keep the work."

I blink blankly, opening my mouth to speak. But I cannot seem to find the right words.

He pushes his hands back into his pockets. "See you around."

I close my hand around the finger guards, and when I look up, Mike is already too far away to hear any reply.

He remembered my finger and cared enough to buy the guards.

Tia runs down the lane, puffing loudly. She reaches my side, bending over to catch her breath. "You left without me."

I shove the leather guards into my skirt pocket. "Sorry."

But Tia is too quick, and she tilts her head, folding her arms in front of her. "What's in your pocket?"

I sigh, pulling out Mike's gift.

Tia examines them in my hand. "And? What is so strange about these? I see women at the factory that use them every day. Some say it protects their fingers."

"Mike gave them to me this morning."

Her mouth falls open, and she scratches her head. "I thought you said Mike and you didn't get along?"

I nod.

She bites the tip of a fingernail, the edges of her mouth rising slightly. She pats my back. "I see. Maybe this is his way of saying sorry."

I cannot seem to smile, even though I know she is teasing me. I look at the leather finger guards once more, trying to understand.

Why did he bring these for me? I made it clear what I thought of him.

"Relax, Stella. It's not like he asked you to go courting. Maybe he just saw your finger and wants to be your friend."

The muscles in my shoulders fall, the tension seeming to slip away. Maybe Tia is right. Maybe he just wants to be my friend.

Eighteen

Nie trzeba dowierzać.
Distrust is the mother of safety.

English sounds are irregular on my lips, and I know the words will never flow fluently from my mouth. Still, I try to speak it with Tia. Some days at the factory, we only speak in English.

These are the quieter days.

Marco has started coming to the café on Saturday mornings to meet Vic and me. He asks when I will go dancing again. He says he still wants a dance with me.

Mike comes along to the café with his brother, too. He is quiet around Vic, always watching me. Sometimes I see a flicker of amusement flash across his eyes when Marco teases me, or a soft shake of his head when he notices how tired I am. Ofttimes, before I can even answer a question, Mike casts a telling expression, as if he knows what I will say.

The Nosic brothers are altogether too unfamiliar. I find myself comparing them to Andrzejek and Oliwjer, though there are little similarities: one set is familiar and safe, the other is new and alarming.

"Marzewska."

I look up from my machine, suddenly aware of Mr. Pruski's hard stare. I stand, keeping my gaze low. "Yes, Mr. Pruski?"

He is a short man, but with very broad shoulders and a belly that hangs over his trousers. His face is made into a permanent scowl, as if he is constantly sucking on a sour grape. It's near impossible to tell whether or not he is angry, or if it's just a part of his features.

He leans against a chair, and I notice the chair legs wobble. I think he is angry this time. His cheeks are red. "Get your mind out of the clouds!" he barks at me.

I stare at the floor and nod.

He is gone within a moment, and the girls at my station break into laughter.

"Get your mind out of the clouds," Tia says, sarcasm coating each word. "And bow to me, while you are at it."

The other women laugh once more.

I give a slight smile. Mr. Pruski is hard on us, but he watches me more. I cannot decide if he likes my work, or if he is waiting for me to make a mistake. "Why does he watch me?" I ask Tia.

"Who knows, Stella? But he is a miserable man, without anything to live for but this job."

"He is married though with children, yes?" I ask.

One of the other girls shakes her head. Lucy has worked here the longest. "His wife has lost her wits," she explains. "Some say it was the passage over, but I think it is the poverty. She went mad trying to make her life better than it was in Poland, only to find her happiness unchanged."

My hands fall to my lap, the garment slipping to the dirty floor.

The woman continues, "Us Poles go from one rule to the next. We might live in America now, but there isn't anything American about us. We live the rule of the factory and streets."

I brush the dirt off the garment. I do not agree, so I stay silent. There is something much worse than having to work, having to struggle—servitude. I have lived without many freedoms, and I cannot compare my life now with what it was before. There is no hope in a situation that cannot change. That is why I left Durliosy, and I see that I am different.

I can do with struggle, but I can't do without my chance to choose tomorrow. I could not live the life assigned to me under Jozef's rule. The only other option was to marry a man that did not truly love me.

I chose this. I chose an opportunity to change my own lot. The work is heavy, but it is not crushing. And more than that, it is my work, my choice. I did not come to America to be rich; I came to be free. And yes, there are different types of freedom. I do not expect to be free of my class or nationality, but I will be free from the rule of another person.

"Eh, Stella, you are about to sew it shut!" Tia yells, waking me from my thoughts.

I wind the needle back quickly, inspecting my mistake.

"What are you thinking so much about?" Tia asks, folding her pile of garments.

I shake my head, hoping to dismiss her curiosity. "Just about how different America is."

Tia and Lucy break into laughter, as if I said something funny.

"What?" I ask.

One of the girls shakes her head, turning away. "You were thinking about that boy, no? The one that always comes by. The younger Nosic boy? Your brother says he is worried Marco is growing fond of you."

"I do not want to think about any man right now. Marco is a boxer, and he smiles too much."

Tia giggles, covering her mouth with her hands. "His brother Mike is also handsome, maybe more handsome. What about him, Stella?"

I shake my head again.

The girls just stare at me in what looks to be disbelief. No one asks me anything else. They just go back to their work, sewing.

I would not want a man that was trained in hitting people. I have been hit far too often to ever wish that upon myself.

The steps down the side of the factory are full of women, young and old, hurrying for their dinner. Tia holds me by the arm, directing me through the chaos.

I hurry my steps, passing Tia. The men from the docks return home at this time too, and I try my best to avoid Marco and Mike. I can't decide why I avoid Mike especially, but I think it is because of my racing heart and the conflicting thoughts that come when I am by him. I cannot see reason around Mike; it is as if my mind is suddenly blurred like the pages of a tiny book.

"Stella! Stella!"

The Nosic brothers are a few strides behind us.

I sigh. I was too slow.

Tia sees the brothers too and she raises her brows.

Marco jogs to catch me. He reaches me, and his greeting is impossible to ignore. "Stella," he says, panting. "I thought it was you."

I swallow, forcing myself to answer back. "Hello, Marco."

He grins. "My brother and I are going to the west side of Fells Point. The Italians make casalinga pizza for cheap. If you haven't tried it, you should come with me. It's not so far, and I could use your company. We could go dancing afterward." Marco is only two years older than me, but he talks as if he is even older.

I am sweating beneath my wool coat, nervous as I always am when he talks to me. "I've just been at work," I say.

"I can see that," Marco says, grinning. "And what are you doing now? Won't you come with me?"

I shrug. "I have clothes to clean and other things I need to do before my day off." The excuse is pathetic, even to my own ears.

Mike has finally caught up with us. His hair is tangled from wearing a cap, a dark smudge across his forehead.

I smile, my eyes directing my amusement.

Mike's hands instantly fly to his hair, alarm evident in his quick movement. Then his eyes meet mine, and I sense a question and a greeting behind his gaze.

Marco talks to Tia, but stops when he hears Mike's "Hello."

"Will you come dancing tonight? My brother says you will never come, but I want to prove him wrong," Marco says.

My shoe sticks in the crack of the sidewalk, and I stumble. I catch myself from falling, but Mike's hand is there, against my back, to steady me.

Marco studies my face, waiting for a response. "Well, Stella?"

"I think maybe another time," I say, biting my lip, still flushed from my stumble.

Mike smiles at his brother, as if he has won some wager, and as usual, my uncharacteristic boldness returns. "On second thought, maybe I do have time for dancing. That is, if Tia will come along."

Tia's eyes gleam, her smile lighting the rest of her face. "That sounds like just the thing after a long week."

Marco slaps his hands together and laughs. "We'll make a good time of it, I can promise you that. Bring Tia, Vic, anyone you like. We'll be at the alley behind our boarding house at seven 'o'clock for dancing."

I smile, pretending to anticipate it, but really I feel sick inside, as if my stomach is in my throat once more.

I steal a glance at Mike.

He is clearly amused, his lips formed into a tight smile.

I stick out my chin a little and make a point to smile extra wide at Marco once more. "I'll look forward to it then."

Marco, finding a blush of his own, says some Croatian phrase and winks. He turns at the next corner, waving goodbye to me.

Just as I guessed, the edges of Mike's lips fall into what only can be considered a frown. Why this makes me satisfied, I am not exactly sure.

"You like my brother, then?" is all he says.

I scan the street for some escape or distraction. Nothing. So, I inhale the musty air. "It depends on what you mean. If you mean that Marco is a friend, then yes. But I am not looking to become anyone's girl."

Mike presses his lips together. His hands are in his pockets, and with his messy hair, he almost looks like a little boy for a moment. Then I realize my head only reaches his chest.

"I think you know how my brother feels. Why did you accept his invitation tonight?"

My chest tightens and I don't respond.

"Do you like teasing him, then?" Mike asks.

I sigh, my bottom lip trembling from the nerves climbing up my throat. "No, I don't want to tease him."

His eyes are glued to my expression.

I lick my lips, fighting the urge to look away. "I saw you. You thought I would not come."

Mike shrugs, and I see the question in his eyes before he speaks it. "So?"

"You don't know me as well as you think you do. I am only just learning how to laugh and dance. It is all new, so different from the old country."

Tia is thankfully distracted, scanning the crowd of men for her father. "Stella, I will try to come tonight." She smiles and squeezes my hand before disappearing in the crowd.

Mike and I walk in silence. The snow from the morning is melted, but the sun is starting to fall behind a cloud now, and the cold temperatures are returning.

Mike puts his hand on my arm, stopping me, and shakes a finger at me. "Maybe you are wrong."

"About what?" I ask, staring at his hand on my arm.

He pulls his hand away, rubbing it along his jaw and the back of his neck. He shakes his head. The lines around his eyes deepen, and his voice becomes quiet. "Maybe I do know you better than you think, and maybe you don't know what you want all the time."

A warm sensation rushes to my arm where he touched me, but I ignore it. I try to ignore how serious his handsome features have become, how his shoulders lean toward me, and how his eyes appear a shade lighter.

I look away. "You can't know someone in so little time."

"Maybe you are right, but maybe not." He clears his throat, lifting his chin. "But I can see you wish I was wrong. What do you have to be so afraid of, Stella? That we might actually get on together, or what? Perhaps that you might actually like spending time with a boxer?"

His face is twisted into a smile, but I can hear the edge in his voice, the way his voice cracked when he said the word *boxer*. And as if my stomach was not already tight, his questions cause my head to spin.

I wrap my arms around my stomach, swallowing the freezing, dry air around me. "It isn't anything like that."

"Then what?"

I shrug. I can't lie more to Mike, so I say nothing. Mania hit me often, and even she didn't unnerve me the way Mike, who has never hit me, does. It must be something more than his boxing that unsettles me, but I cannot understand it. Maybe it is the way he speaks to me, the way he can't seem to sugarcoat anything. It feels as if he can see right through me—his words, like daggers, land much too close to my heart. I swallow, recognizing what it is about Mike unnerves me.

He is too close, too close to uncovering everything about my past that I have tried so desperately to hide. He is too close to seeing me as I am—the reasons I do the things I do, says the things I say. I cannot bear to be seen, not yet, not when I feel so new to freedom.

Mike's posture is rigid, his eyes resting on the ground in front of him. I can see a layer of dirt on his cheeks, a few clear lines running down his face where the sweat of the day must have dripped. He turns toward me. "Well, I guess I'll be seeing you tonight—dancing."

I nod, pulling my collar around my neck.

He walks backward, watching me. "Oh, and one more thing, Stella."

I lift my chin. "Yes?"

Mike smiles, and I notice the freckle above his lip once more. "I hope you'll dance with me this time." His eyes meet mine, and the dark color somehow seems warmer again, the corner of his eyes wrinkling in unison with the edges of his lips. He pushes one hand through his hair. "Well?"

I swallow and nod, trying to ignore my sudden breathlessness, the sudden strong desire to be closer to him. "Maybe."

"Well then, Stella," he says, "See you around, *maybe*."

He disappears into the maze of streets and people, leaving me alone to wander back to my boarding house. My legs carry me home, but my mind remains at that street corner with Mike.

A tingling sensation still burns along my arm where Mike touched me. My pulse is uneven, my body suddenly numb to the chilling temperature around me. And yet somehow, I feel a little more alive.

The dance is near the Broadway Market, right across from the fish market. Though the building is clean, it's small, and the group of fifty or so dancers almost fill the room when spread out.

In my short time in America, I have stayed in east Fells Point. It is like a Polish town—the shops run by Poles, the factory run by Poles, and even the churches conducting their services in Polish. And though I cannot read the many signs around the city, I recognize they, too, are written in a Slavic language. It's easier this way.

Many say the road to becoming American is long and hard. So, we start in our own community, our own city away from our country, and those that aren't Polish—like the Croatians—have their own community, or at least know how to navigate the Polish customs and language.

But in this small building, there are musicians playing Croatian folk music. It surprises me how much this music, compared to the music of the other dances, reminds me of the songs at the festivals in Ostroleka. There is no accordion, but the sound of the samica and gunjac and voices singing together lift my spirits.

I close my eyes, sensing I am truly in Poland again.

Music has a way of transporting us places, sometimes even to places we do not wish to return to.

I am paired with Marco and he swings me around to the music, sometimes skipping to the side as we go. Every now and again, he pulls his arms from my waist to clap in unison with the others.

The dancing and singing from the old country calm me. I do not wish to think of the past, but somehow being with others who have experienced at least some of what I have brings comfort. I am not alone in this new world of America.

Tia dances with Mike. She laughs at each unexpected turn, her face coloring when she bumps into the couple beside her.

"So, Stella," Marco begins, raising a brow at me. "Is it much different than the way you danced in Poland?"

I smile, but only shrug.

He laughs. "I do not think you will ever speak more than one sentence to me at a time."

I smile again. He might be right. And when the song ends, and Tia and Mike return to our side, I exhale in relief.

Tia grins at me. "I thought I knew how to dance."

"Maybe Mike should learn to lead better," Marco says, nudging his older brother with an elbow to the ribs.

Tia says something in response, perhaps a bit funny.

But I am not listening anymore. A deep baritone voice fills the room, the strings strumming softly. It is a slower song, and the singer is talented.

There's a gentle tug of my hands, and I open my eyes to see Mike pulling me toward the other dancers.

He smiles at me. "You like the song?"

That strange burning in my chest returns. "It's beautiful."

Mike's shoulders fall. "It reminds me of home."

I shrug, blowing a stray hair from my face. "Home? Do you still think of the old country as home?"

Marco has pulled Tia next to us, casting a dark glare at Mike.

Mike doesn't seem to notice his brother, or if he does, he doesn't seem to care. He still stares at me. His hand on my back pulls me closer, perhaps in response to Marco's expression.

"Why did you come to America?" I ask him.

Mike leans closer, shaking his head. "For many reasons. My mother begged us not to, but we had hardly anything to eat. With so many little brothers and sisters, we needed more.

"Why does anyone come to America? We were starving and poor. Marco and I came to earn money, to support our family." He stops, narrowing his eyes. A faint smile spreads across his face, "But I am going back, once I earn enough to take home."

My eyes widen. "I will never go back."

Mike's jaw juts forward, and my eyes trace the pattern of stubble on his chin and cheeks. "Not even for your mother or father, Stella?"

"No," I say, bitterness seeping out.

"My mother is very ill. She begs me to come back so that she can see me once more." Mike pauses, and the strings become louder. "Why did you come?"

I try to collect my thoughts, but before I catch myself, I am talking, saying much more than I ever intended to tell anybody. "I have been motherless since before I can remember. My father died long ago too. The Russians that occupied our country would not even let us speak Polish at school. So I had to quit school—I didn't know enough Russian to get by. But even worse, if we showed any kind of Polish pride, there were consequences. Most people, like me, couldn't see the point of fighting back. We had nothing. The harder we worked, the more the landholders took. My father died fighting against it. My older brother took me in. He married a Croatian."

Mike leans forward again. "That is why you speak Croatian?"

"Yes, but she was not kind; they were not kind. Everyone else escaped—my brother Vic and Stan came here, Franz chose the church, and Amalia married. And I was stuck there, nothing left for me. Vic sent my passageway. So that is how I came."

"Hmm," he says, scanning my expression. "And how old are you?" he asks.

"Sixteen," I say, but then I realize my birthday was a week ago. "No, seventeen. Seventeen just eight days ago."

One side of Mike's lips rise. "You forgot your birthday?"

I blow the hair from my face again and sigh. "What is a birthday but a date? It means nothing to me except that I have lived another year on this earth."

Mike frowns. "You do not celebrate?"

"Celebrate? You sound like a rich American." I laugh out loud. "You did not say how old you are?"

"Twenty-two," he says.

"Mike," I say, my voice cracking. "What is your real name—the name you were called in the old country?"

He spins me, pulling me closer afterward. "Marion."

He touches my face, wiping the stubborn hair behind my ear. I feel the heat in my face, the pit in my stomach. His fingers trace the outline of my cheek down to my chin before his arm falls back to my waist.

Mike chuckles. "So serious all the time. Don't you like to laugh?"

I nod. "When there is something to laugh about. But life has a way of being so serious."

"Ah, but don't you see? Life is always serious. You don't have to be."

The music comes to an end. I feel disappointed and relieved, a strange mixture of emotions I never thought possible. But then again, I keep finding new feelings that I've never experienced.

I wonder if it's America. I wonder if it's Mike.

Marco is beside us in an instant. He whispers something to his brother, and Mike rolls his eyes.

I seize the moment to grab Tia's hands and pull her toward the dancing circle. Anything to distract myself from the tension of the Nosic brothers.

Nineteen

Prawda w winie.
In wine there is truth.

Vic waits outside my boarding house, a glass bottle near his feet. He is so ornery when he is drunk. He sits on the steps, staring into the darkness.

"Vic," I say. "Where is your coat?"

Vic's eyes roll backward. "You missed an exciting game." He laughs, then bites the side of his cheek. "Do you know what happened? Can you guess? I never lose when I play cards, you know. You remember meeting my friend—he will tell you I never lose. I only bet when I win. But this night," he stops, hiccuping and laughing once more. "This night, I lost."

I shift my weight, looking from Tia to Mike. "Yes? Well, we can talk about that in the morning, Vic. Let's get you home" I say, pulling at his arm to help him up.

He swats my arm away. "But I want to talk about it right now."

I give Mike a pleading look, hoping he will know what to do. He nudges Marco, and the pair of them lift Vic off the steps.

All the while, Vic keeps saying, "Get your hands off me! I can walk myself."

In truth, he can hardly hold himself up, so Marco and Mike ignore his protests.

I wave my hand at them. "Don't worry, Vic is not the violent type. He just complains and yells. He won't be too much of a problem."

"What good is a little sister who acts like my mother?" my brother asks, his face turning red.

"Stop it, Vic. You must go to home and get to bed. Everything will make more sense in the morning.

"You stop it," he says, spitting as he speaks. "I have lost everything. Soon, I won't have a place to stay. I do not have enough money for rent. You'll have to bail me out. You might even have to marry that Marco. I cannot take care of you." He stops, glancing at Marco. Then, Vic smiles, his eyes rolling backward. "Just as I won your ticket, I've lost. What goes around comes around, Stella."

I shake my head, staring at his sloppy dress. The top buttons of his shirt are undone, and his shirt hangs over his trousers, only tucked in around one side. His hair is poking straight up on one side, the result of his hands combing through it over and over and over again.

"I have money of my own, Vic. You do not take care of me," I say, shaking my head. "If you are in trouble, I can help you. Let me help with your rent."

Vic laughs, slurring his words, "I'll take your money. You go from one brother to the next, maybe you will go to another man like that Croatian boxer, like an old hat. You have nothing of your own. You are only a girl."

My eyes dart upward. I know he doesn't mean it. He is talking nonsense, but something tells me there is some truth in it.

Tia grabs my hand, tears springing to her eyes. "Your brother needs a good slap," she whispers.

I shake my head, looking at my feet. "He is only drunk. This is not him."

Tia's expression softens, her light green eyes glistening. "The drink loosens the tongue."

I pull my hand from hers and rush to Mike's side. "Mike, can you and Marco manage him?"

"We'll get him home," Mike says, placing one hand against my back. "What about you? Will you be alright?"

I straighten, thankful he cannot see the tears building behind my eyes. "I'll be fine. Thank you for your help."

"Don't mention it," he says, draping one of Vic's arms around his neck.

Vic stumbles forward, his chin dropping toward his chest.

I remain on the pavement, watching their figures disappear. A few snowflakes are floating in the air, the light from the lanterns reflecting on the flecks. Tia stands beside me, but says nothing.

The alcohol has clouded his mind. Vic is kinder than that, softer than that. But the drink makes him different, almost like Jozef. He said he won my passage here. I do not doubt it. I wondered before how he paid it.

There is always a loser in gambling, in drinking. Vic won my passage on a bet, effectively eliminating someone else's passage. But he lost tonight, so much more than money. Perhaps Stan was right to leave Vic.

What's worse is that Vic's words stung. Maybe Tia is right—maybe the drink just loosens the tongue. But am I really just an object to be passed around from one man to the next—from father to brother to brother to husband?

Does a woman have no power of her own?

I want my own power, my own life, my own money, my own future. I thought it was different here, with Vic, but maybe it isn't. Maybe he was just waiting for me to make money for him.

My chest tightens, a physical pain spreading throughout my body.

It can't be true. Not with Wiktor. Maybe with this new Vic, desperate for alcohol and gambling and money. Maybe Vic is not the Wiktor I knew before.

I crack an eye open, the sound of creaking floorboards stirring me from the restless sleep. I spent the night in silence, fighting the urge to cry. My body begged for sleep, yet my mind, much like the clock at the bedside, was wound too tight and spun from thought to thought, replaying everything that Vic had said.

Tia is at the mirror, splashing her face with water. She turned in her covers for most of the night. I suspect she slept little.

Slipping from the covers, I step down from the bunk, my legs shaking.

Tia dries her face with a rag, but she stops when our eyes meet. The edges of her lips rise, but it is a weak attempt. "How did you sleep?"

I shrug.

"Your brother is waiting for you outside. One of the girls came and told me," she says.

"Here?"

She nods.

Without a hesitation, I wrap my coat around my nightclothes and pull my savings from my purse.

"Stella," Tia calls, following me past the door. "What will you say to him?"

It's the same question that I asked all night. I lick my lips, wrapping my arms around my stomach. "I'm not sure, but I have to make sure this does not happen again."

She smiles, but the lightness in her eyes has darkened to a gray, the bags beneath signaling her sleepless night. She wraps her arms around my neck. "You are a good sister, and Vic is good to you. You will work it out."

Tia always knows what to say, and I thank her, returning her embrace.

"Good luck," she says, retreating.

I could not leave Durliosy without facing Franz, and I cannot move forward without confronting Vic. Amidst discomfort, I press onward.

The sun seeps through the open door, a stark contrast to the dark hallway.

Vic leans against a post, rousing when he meets my eye. He is wearing the same clothes as the night before, though this time his shirt is buttoned and tucked into his trousers. I am relieved to see he has combed his disheveled hair; at least he made an attempt to groom himself.

"Stella," he says, swallowing hard. The lines near his mouth deepen, his lips creasing together. A trolley car approaches, dinging as it halts. Vic grabs at his temples, reeling forward.

There is a certain loudness in silence, an echoing of sentiments. Sadness, anger, disappointment—these ring much louder than words spoken.

He breaks the stillness, unable to withstand it. "I was drunk, but not so drunk that I don't remember some of what was said. I said things I shouldn't have."

Tears prick my eyes, the injustice assailing my heart afresh. I feel his gaze, but I cannot meet it.

"I am sorry. We'll find a way to weather this. Even if it means I go to the mines. I won't let you be ruined, not when it is all my fault." His voice cracks, succumbing to emotion.

I hold out my purse.

There is not much I can say. I have only questions—more questions than I could ever ask him, more than he could answer. There are so many. I settle for just one. "When were you going to tell me you gambled my money too?"

Vic's face twists in agony, his eyes reducing to slits. He stumbles backward, faltering against the brick. He shakes his head but does not answer.

"Vic, there are few things in life that are mine. But this—this money," I say, tossing it at his feet, "I work for every day. I don't work for you or a husband or brother or sister. I work for me. You must not ever claim me or the few things I have as yours again. If you do, I promise you, I will leave just as Stanislaus did. I will do whatever it takes to be free of this."

He nods, tears choking him.

"We are even now. I've repaid my passage."

I leave without another word, slamming the house door, determined to prevent his sobs from softening my resolve.

Tia's eyes widen when I return and collapse on my bed. "Stella," is all she says, climbing the bunk to comfort me.

I say a silent prayer that God is watching over me still, leading me on a journey much farther than I anticipated before. I pray God is leading me to true freedom.

Twenty

Dobre daleko słychać, a złe jeszcze dalej.
Good deeds are remembered but bad
ones are etched in our memory

There are days that never end, factory shifts that morph into eternities, work so numbing I lose sensibility. In these instances, I drift to the place I have sworn to forget.

Durliosy.

Many days, I am pulling the cart to market again, and it's not just a memory. I am there, reliving it over and over again—the thrust of wind, my frozen toes, the forgotten path ahead. I struggle under the weight of the cart, wishing for Andrzejek and Oliwjer to stop once more and carry me.

Sometimes, Franz chases me, warning me of danger and dishonesty; Jozef and Mania—the consequences of my departure.

Then there is Bronia, the one memory I cling to. It has been less than five months since I saw her last, yet the details of her face fade. Sometimes I close my eyes and pray to God that I can recall her face—her eyes, her voice, her crooked teeth—one last time.

Maybe even she is angry. Yet something tells me she forgives me, that she knew all along I would not be hers forever. She found the branches, and she knew. She knew I loved her.

That is what I tell myself.

These vivid deliberations always end in the same question: Am I still pulling the cart to market—maybe not the cart itself, but the pain, the faces, the memories? Will someone find me, see it is too heavy to bear? I wish, even pray, for relief from the weight, to sit by a friend and rest my eyes for part of the journey.

The treat, wrapped in white paper and a pink bow, smells of chocolate and berries.

"Well?" Mike says, shrugging a shoulder.

"What's this for?" I ask. We haven't spoken for a week, not since Vic was drunk.

"It's for your birthday, your birthday a few weeks ago," Mike says, leaning to smell the wrapped treat. His eyes widen, and he smiles. "It's cake."

I nod, smiling. "I know what it is," I say, taking a bite. "Thank you."

He smiles back, his temples creasing. "Look," he says, backing a few steps. "I've got to get back." He turns to the corner, rubbing his right arm.

"You have a match tonight?" I ask.

He nods, his brows wrinkling together. "But you don't like that?" he asks.

He knows I don't.

Mike kicks a pebble, and it jumps across the pavement. He rubs his arm again. "I don't like to fight, Stella, but it brings good money, more than I make a week at the loading docks."

My shoulders tense, and I wrap and set the cake in my pocket. I don't want to argue. "Someone always loses. It doesn't seem fair."

Fair. Deserve. Since when did I consider what is fair, what is deserved?

Mike kicks another stone so hard it flies clear across the street. "I never gamble," he says. "Boxing is different. It is a sport, a competition. My brother and I are a team. We have loyalties in the club—people root for us."

"You mean they bet on you," I say, shifting my weight.

Mike's eyes darken. "I don't think I'm a bad boxer to bet on. Besides, there are worse things than boxing—things like starving, dying, or even servitude," he says, his tone laced with a warning. "I will always do what I have to do. It isn't about morals, Stella."

There isn't anything else to say, for we won't reach an agreement, at least not today, and I won't argue more. Perhaps Mike is right, but I've lost everything from Vic's gambling.

I smile, nudging him with my elbow. "Thank you for the cake. I'll think about what you said," is all I can manage.

His hand brushes mine. "Sometimes, Stella, it's worth the risk. No one wins every time, but isn't that life? Shouldn't you try for something more?"

"I thought you said you don't gamble." I say, casting him a reproachful glare.

He laughs. "I'm not talking about cards or boxing, Stella. I'm talking about something much more serious."

The lines around his eyes deepen, his gaze softening.

I pull my scarf across my cheek, hoping Mike won't see the blush. "You better get to your match."

He tilts his head, smiling. "See you around."

"Mike, c'mon," Marco yells from the corner. He squints, blocking his eyes from the sun. "Hey, Stella!"

I wave, then turn to Mike. "Good luck."

He says goodbye, running to meet his brother.

Two brothers again, but this time I prefer the older one.

Twenty-One

Jakie pytanie, taka odpowiedź.
Just as one calls into the forest, so it echoes back.

It's the fourth Sunday of Lent, and the Broadway Market has transformed. The bright flowers, the musicians, the scent of pierogi, sausages, and breads—it is the beginning of a new season, the ending of the winter.

Children run around, Marzanna dolls in hand, awaiting the procession.

A Nosic brother stands on each side of me, the morning a series of awkward interactions with the competing brothers.

"Tell me, Stella, why do they carry the dolls?" Marco asks, putting his arm around my shoulders.

I shrug his arm away, stepping toward a group of children. "It's an old pagan Polish tradition. Marzanna is winter or death, so when we drown Marzanna, we beckon spring to come."

Mike laughs. "So you drown a doll?"

I turn to him, glaring.

He is still chuckling, his head shaking back and forth.

"It's symbolic," I say, nudging him with an elbow, "and it isn't always death by water. Sometimes we burn the dolls. But Marzanna represents so much more than just winter. It represents all the bad things winter brings, like illness, death, and sadness. When Marzanna is gone, there is finally room for sunshine, goodness, and health."

Mike's smile falls, confusion replacing humor. "But why celebrate in such a pagan way? Why not just a feast?"

I smile. "The tradition started before Christian rites. It's only for fun now."

Marco pulls at my arm, putting more distance between me and Mike. "It makes sense to me, Stella. Such things are tradition. Besides, I wouldn't mind lighting a rag doll on fire."

"Let's make one," I say, motioning to a booth with assorted rags and straw.

Tia steps forward, her eyes lighting. "I haven't made one in ages. I hardly remember."

"You can't mess it up," I say, handing her a piece of fabric.

I loop my rag around and around—a knot for the head and chest, strings for the arms and legs. Adding sprigs of straw to the top, I stand back, showing Tia.

Tia and I join in the singing, and eventually, we make our way to the water's edge with the procession, each of us holding a Marzanna rag doll. Some light their dolls on fire before throwing them into the sea.

I hold mine at arm's length, remembering my childhood in Durliosy once more. The darkness of winter had always been so literal to me, so tied to the actual seasons and sun. Now, however, I celebrate the death of a season of life—a season of darkness and struggle.

I wipe a joyful tear and toss the effigy into the sea. At first it floats, but my Marzanna eventually fills with water, the sea swallowing it whole.

Mike leans over the ledge, peering beneath the water.

"You can't look back," I say, "it's bad luck."

He scrunches his nose and clicks his tongue. "Superstitions," he says, offering a side smile.

Tia wraps her arm around my waist, pulling me back to the procession. We sing all the way back to the Broadway Market, arm in arm. The singing turns to dancing, and Mike grabs my hand, pulling me into the square.

His eyes bear into mine, sending my heart racing. "Do you want to get out of here?" he asks.

I startle. "And do what? Leave Tia and Marco?"

He nods, grinning. "I want to show you something. Will you come with me? Just for an hour, and then we can come back here. Marco and Tia won't even notice we're gone."

It takes all effort not to laugh. "Marco won't notice?"

He lifts one brow, a mischievous glint playing across his eyes. "Well, he probably will, but a moment with you is worth it, Stella."

Blood rushes to my cheeks. "Alright, but let's be quick."

Mike nods, clasping his hand over mine. The warmth of his touch envelops me, and we weave between the dancers, escaping Marco's sight.

I laugh, surprised again at how alive I feel.

He moves quickly, leading me through and past the market.

I can hardly keep up with him. "Where are you taking me?" I ask, trying to slow him down.

Mike stops, bending over to catch his breath. His deep laughter brings a smile to my cheeks. "Oh just a few blocks more, but I suppose we could walk." He pauses, breath staggering. "That Marco is difficult to ward away."

I welcome the change of pace, my heart still racing from the exercise.

"I think we lost them. Even if Marco saw us leave, I don't think he could have followed us." He glances over his shoulder. "I am sorry about Marco. I can't seem to persuade him to leave you alone."

I shrug. "I'm not sure why he pays me so much attention."

Mike grasps my arm, a smirk spreads across his cheeks. "Come on, you can't tell me that. That's fishing, if I ever heard."

I cast him a reproaching glance. "I'm serious. It's not as if I've encouraged him. I hardly speak to him, and still he comes around."

Mike's jaw drops, his expression softening. "Ah, so you don't know then?"

I shake my head.

When I say nothing, he leans closer and whispers, "You're beautiful."

Some girls, like Tia or Amalia, would know how to respond to Mike, but I don't. I say nothing, hoping the blush will die down. The shock must register, for he doesn't push the issue further.

Instead, Mike tugs at my hand again, pulling me toward a railing. "Come on, Stella, this is it."

I follow him up the steps. They climb high above the street, back and forth and over the five floors to the roof. From the roof's edge, I can see much of Fells Point. The market seems small from here, the water in the distance a glowing silver light.

"Is this what you wanted to show me?" I ask, pointing toward the view below.

Mike reaches into his coat. "Partly." He pulls out a bottle of wine. "And, I wanted to show you this."

I bite the inside of my cheek, stepping backward. "Are you trying to get me drunk?"

Mike's deep laughter returns, and his eyes are watery from the exertion. "No, nothing like that. I've been saving this bottle for some time."

"What are you saving it for?" I ask, staring at the way Mike cradles the bottle.

Mike's features fall. "I don't know." He repositions himself on the wall of the roof, stretching his legs and turning the bottle around in his hands. "This is special wine, all the way from my home—Lovrec, Croatia."

I nod, still confused at his reason for bringing me here.

"I helped my father and uncles make this wine, and then I carried it across the ocean. I keep thinking I'll drink it, but I can't."

"You made it?" I ask, urging him forward.

He nods. "In Croatia, we make wine. Our vineyard is small, but we always have enough wine for our family, and a little to sell." He sighs, setting the bottle down. "I wanted to share that with you, a piece of my past. I was hoping you might share something with me. Don't you miss anything about the old country?"

"Some things, but not many."

Mike stares down below. "I wish I could bring my whole country to America. I miss the ways, my family, the sea."

"But there is water here," I say, pointing to the horizon.

He shakes his head. "It's not the same type of sea." His eyes gloss over, his gaze fading to the horizon. I can see a part of his heart is still across the water.

"You do not wish to forget, then?"

He turns towards me, his dark eyes meeting mine. "Today was the first time I saw a bit of the old country in you. Why do you wish to forget?"

I twist my fingers around my braid, hoping to find the right words. "It isn't easy to explain, Mike. It was one thing after another in Poland, always something to make life harder. If it wasn't family, it was the Russian soldiers. If it wasn't them, then it was starvation, a blow to the face, a broken heart." My voice cracks, and suddenly emotion claws at my throat. "And the worst part is that in order to leave it behind, I had to leave the one person I loved most in the world, my little niece."

Mike only stares at me, his breathing turning shallow. He touches my hand.

I wipe at the tears by my eyes, shaking my head. "It's not worth talking about."

He stands up, tucking the bottle inside his coat. "I didn't mean to upset you. Should we go back? I'm sure they are still dancing."

I nod, and he helps me to my feet.

"Stella," he says, his voice softer. "I can't understand how something so beautiful came from such sorrow."

Once again, I shrug, aware of the burning sensation in my chest. I glance up at his face, tracing the outline of his features with my eyes. "Thank you," I say, trying to ignore the beating of my heart.

We stand there in silence. Below us, the market is busy and loud, the streets filled with people from the festival. Yet it is quiet and comforting standing on the roof with Mike.

He steps closer and his hand brushes mine. At first I think it unintentional, but then I see his thumb graze the back of my hand again.

My eyes dart to his, my mouth suddenly dry.

Mike takes my hand in his. "Is this alright?"

Somehow, his calloused hands seem soft, gentle even. My heart races at the touch. He held it before, leading me to the rooftop. Yet standing here, hand in hand, seems more significant.

I clear my throat and nod, not finding the right words.

Mike grins, and for the first time, I allow myself to study his handsome features. He chuckles at my gawking, and pulls me toward the stairs. "We better get back, or Marco will have it out with me later."

He squeezes my hand, leading me back.

Twenty-Two

Więcej ludzi utonęło w kieliszku niż w morzu.
Wine has drowned more than the sea.

The late afternoon skies show no signs of darkening. The snow has melted. Everything is still brown, but the small green patches in the grass signal that it won't be long until the leaves return.

In a month or two, the fields of poppies in Durliosy will be blooming. I remember the vivid red of the flowers, the tall grass growing in between. Once they bloom, Bronia will be there, picking the flowers for a crown of red.

My walk from the factory feels shorter now that it is warmer. I add an extra block on especially pleasant days like today. I walk by the café and laundry shop, pausing by the Turnbol house.

Sometimes Mike is here, about to start a match, and he'll come and talk with me. He always has a smile for me, tells me something to brighten my day, and I leave feeling as if he has inched even closer to my heart.

But he is not there today; no one is. The perimeter of the building is bare, and the shutters are closed. The usual shouts and jeerings, the rowdiness, the men smoking by the door—all of it is removed.

It's strange to see the building so alone, so abandoned. It used to bother me, but I've grown accustomed to it, and the unexpected change feels eerie.

A breeze brushes my cheek, and I turn my head, shielding my face from the wind. That's when I see the dark figure crouching near the corner of the club. He sits against the brick façade, nearly shaded from view. I squint, just as he leans forward, and the afternoon glow lights his face.

His eye is swollen shut, and there is dried blood splattered across his head and clothes. Cuts mark his oppressor's blows, bruises purpling the top of his cheekbone.

I nearly trip on the ledge of the pavement, lurching forward. "Marco?" I say, running to his side. "What has happened?"

He stares at me, an odd glint in his eyes. "I will never speak to him again."

He stands, pushing past me toward the entrance of the club.

"Marco, tell me what has happened," I say, my voice cracking. "You're hurt, you need help. What happened?"

He stops, his back still facing me, his hand clutching the handle of the door. "Perhaps you should ask your brother, Vic."

I stand there for only a moment after he leaves, trying to make sense of what I saw, what I heard.

My leisure walk turns hurried, each step becoming more impatient as I navigate the streets. It's as if my racing heart alone carries my feet along the path.

I don't even knock. The window has been left open, the breeze chilling my already shaken frame. I close it, the image of Marco's beaten and swollen face springing back to my mind.

Then I hear a soft, tapping sound against the concrete floor. I turn to see my brother sitting on the floor, the tip of his head just visible from the line of the bed.

"Vic," I say, startling in surprise. I go to him, kneeling beside him.

His eyes are swollen, but unlike Marco, it is not from boxing. He has been crying. His shoulders are slumped, and his face is white.

I close my eyes, leaning my head on the bed. What has he lost this time? His debts took most of my savings, and I've only recently begun to recover.

"You did not go to work today?" I ask, trying to ease the tension.

Vic shakes his head, watching my every move.

"You gambled again?" I say, a sharpness in my tone.

Silence.

"I take it the stakes were higher this time?" I ask. My voice shakes.

More silence. His lip trembles.

I speak louder. "Vic? Tell me what happened. You look as if you are standing on your own grave."

He slides to the floor, his figure crumbling to a ball. He wraps his arms around his knees, rocking back and forth.

My heart catches, then leaps forward, as if it will never stop. "Tell me, Vic. I cannot take your silence."

Vic scoots away from me, cowering like a small dog, whimpering.

I curse silently. He must have lost dreadfully.

Cradling his head to my shoulder, I stroke his messy head of hair, and my anger melts to concern, my worry to compassion. "Vic, you can tell me."

He pulls back, shaking his head. "No, Stella, I don't know if I can. That is, you'll know the truth, one way or another, and I don't expect you to ever speak to me again after you do. I've lost you."

I shake my head nervously, inching toward him. "Vic, we've made it before, we can make it through any—"

"There is no us, Stella, not anymore. You'll likely not claim me as a brother, for I haven't acted as such."

I stand, moving to the wash bowl. My face, normally startled by the cold water, is numb. I close my eyes, wiping them with the towel. I blink away the tears sprouting. "Vic, you must tell me everything."

Vic sighs, and from the corner of my eye I see him sit up. He leans against the wall, tossing his head backward. "Stella, I promise I never meant you harm. It started last night at the cards. I had wagered most of my week's earnings and lost. I knew what that did to us last time, and I had promised myself it would never happen again. But there I was, sitting at the table, looking at my losses. Marco and Mike had been fighting. I should have bet on them instead, but I had taken to cards, you see.

"Marco seemed to sense my misfortune, and he came to my table. He placed his winnings from the fight on the table. He wanted in." Vic stops, letting out a miserable moan. "The other men took one look at Marco and left. They don't like to play cards with the boxers. It makes them nervous."

I turn, forcing myself to face Vic, and whatever news he brings, fully. "What next, Vic? What next?" I ask.

Vic shakes his head again, despair written in each shudder and bubbling tear. He closes his eyes and swallows, gesturing with his hands. "We got into a heated game, you see. I told Marco there was nothing left I could give. I was already in the hole far further than before. I was ruined. Well, Marco seemed right pleased about that. In fact, I think he laughed.

"He asked me, 'What if there is a way out?' I told him I didn't know what he meant. He said that there was something he wanted more than money. He told me if I won the last hand of cards that he would forgive me all my debt, but if he won, he wanted—he wanted . . ."

Vic's breathing staggers.

I pour a glass of water, offering it to him.

He drinks it, water dripping down his already moistened chest. His wheezing is worse, and he shakes his head frantically, begging me to leave him.

"Vic. You cannot keep this in. Tell me what happened. Finish this."

A few more minutes of uncomfortable wheezing. It finally slows. "He wanted me to wager you, Stella, as a prize."

I stare at Vic in disbelief. "You can't be serious, Vic. Is that why you fought him?"

Vic drops his head into his hands. "Oh, Stella. I wish it were that simple. When Mike heard about it, he said he wanted in the game too.

"You know I always win. It was a strange night, and I thought if I had one more chance to get us out of the hole, I could do it. I have a knack for the game, and I never thought you were truly in danger—"

"What?" I ask, interrupting him and jerking backward. "You mean to say that you, that you actually wagered me as a prize, as if I were a few chips you could toss into the center of the table?" My face is burning now, but I hold it in still, knowing there is more I must know.

Vic restrains my shoulders, as if I would attack him.

I think I might.

"You don't understand, Stella. I thought if I just had one more chance, I could see us right. I didn't want to drag you down to anything worse." He swallows, closing his eyes. "But then the cards were dealt, and the round began. Straight away, four of a kind, sevens. I felt my courage climbing. I knew we'd be alright, you see."

I shake my head, and the tears begin to pass down my cheek once more.

"Marco lays his hand down all proud like, as if he stacked the deck or something. Nines. Four nines. I could have sworn he planned it. He tells me to take some of the money still, that he got a better deal winning you, but then Mike lays his cards down. Royal flush."

My heart plummets to my gut. Mike? I had thought there was an understanding between him and me. I thought he knew how I felt about gambling. A sudden brokenness becomes me, as if I am standing below the loft again.

I had almost dared to care for him.

"Well, Marco didn't like this, and I promise, neither did I. Though I will say you got the better of the brothers. Marco says, 'You cheat!' to Mike, and pretty soon a real fight breaks out—not the boxing we all usually watch, but a full-on man-versus-man fight. Nobody dared stop them. Never had the Nosic brothers fought each other, and they threw the ugliest jabs and punches I've seen . . . and well, you saw the outcome. Marco lost."

It takes everything in me not to strike Vic. I know it wouldn't do any good, but for the first time, I wish to inflict pain. I clasp my hands behind my back, steadying myself.

"To think you supposed you could bet on me," I say, anger seeping through each word. "No betting of yours can bind me to a man I don't choose. I'll tell you what you're going to do, Vic. You'll find Mike. Tell him the deal is off."

Vic shakes his head, a sheepish shrug his reply. "I can't, Stella. We shook on it."

I almost choke laughing. "You can't bind anything of that nature with a handshake. You really would have me marry Mike because of a bet?"

The silence stings. Vic pulls himself to the window, struggling to open it, his hands trembling. The breeze blows in, sending the few papers on the table floating.

"Vic."

He sobs again. "Stella, I don't want to end up like Marco. I won't fight Mike about it. It's unfair, yes—cruel even—but it was a bet. I'm your guardian, and this is how it will be. Marry Mike. You'll be finally free of me and my ways."

"Then I will speak to him." I turn toward the door, dropping the glass of water to the floor. It shatters into a hundred pieces. "And, yes, Vic. Either way, I will be free of you and your ways, but this is not how it will go. Not like this, not now."

I bang on the door again and again, until my knuckles ache and a passerby takes notice.

I lean against his door, my choked sobs dripping over my boots. There is nothing left to do but wait. I can't turn away, not now, not when so much depends upon this meeting.

"Are you alright, Miss?" a man asks, crouching down beside me. "Can I help you?"

I shake my head, then bury it in my hands. "No."

No one can help me but myself.

"Cheer up," he says before leaving.

It feels like hours before I see Mike's outline against the light of lantern. I stand, tucking my hair behind my ears, thankful my tears are gone.

He sees me, and his steps slow. He stops a few feet away from me, removing his cap. The silence is thick, and I wonder what he could possibly have to say in his defense. To have bet on me, like I was nothing more than a possession. I grit my teeth. I had thought he cared.

"Stella, won't you come in?" he asks, motioning to his door.

My face is hot with anger, but I follow him into the apartment. It's unkept, and I sneer at the mess.

"Please, sit," Mike says, grasping my shoulders and guiding me to a chair. He stands over me, his dark eyes filled with concern. "Out with it. I can see you are upset—like a tiger, ready to pounce."

My chest burns. How can he act so innocent? "I have heard everything. You think you have won me as a wager, but it isn't true. It could never be."

He pulls out another chair, sitting across from me, and reaches for my hand. "You think I won you so that I might own you?"

I rip my hand from his grip, crossing my arms in front of me. I don't understand why he questions me. I want answers.

"Stella, I saw that Marco was set on you, and he would have forced Vic in one way or another," he says, cranking his neck to meet my eyes. "I didn't bet on you. I bet for you. I couldn't let you lose what you have fought so hard for."

"And how would you know what I have fought for? You barely know me," I say, tears stealing from my eyes. "I thought you knew my opinion on gambling, knew how I despised it. To think I had almost—" I stop, pulling to a stand and turning my back to him.

"I see much more than you think. I see you have fought for your independence, your freedom."

"And you would take that away from me?" I ask, bewildered.

"No, never," he says, his voice cracking.

I don't want to believe he is as bad as Marco or Vic. I want to believe he knows me, that he cares. It takes all my courage, but I meet his eye. There isn't a hint a mockery behind his dark eyes, not a thread of deceit.

I wipe my tears. "What do you mean, you fought for me?"

Mike lifts his hands. "I thought that with all the bets for your future, you should have a say. So, I got in, hoping to spare you from the others."

He looks to me, his expression fixed in resolve.

I inhale, my anger beginning to drain. "So, you don't wish to make me marry you?" I ask, trembling. "You don't intend to force me or Vic to do anything?"

Mike shakes his head, and I see he feels the slight of my question. "You think I would do that?"

I hoped he wouldn't, that he hadn't. I look to the ground, not wanting to answer. "You fought your brother?" I ask, trying to change the subject. I sit in the chair once more.

"Yes, and I'd fight yours, too, if I had to," he says. His eyes trace my features, resting on my tear-stained cheeks.

I sigh. "And now you would like my gratitude?" I ask, shaking my head. "That's impossible. I am not a chip in the game. I can't forgive my brother for this, and I don't feel gratitude."

Mike rises, pacing in front of me. "Stella, I would never force you, but I do ask you." He swallows, his cheeks reddening. "You'd be free of Vic and Marco. I offer you freedom. I'm leaving for Lovrec. I am going back, at least for some time."

Marry Mike? Confusion encompasses me, and I brace myself. I don't know if someone can offer anyone else freedom. Freedom is something earned, not given.

"Promise you'll think on it, Stella?" he asks.

"After all that I have been through, all that I have fought, how could you believe I would give up my independence so carelessly? As if I were to run to you, to have you rescue me." I dig my heels into the floor, moving toward the door.

"Stella?" he says, more strongly this time. "That isn't what I meant. I want to marry you."

I can't look to him, not when my heart has been ripped into pieces. I had thought he betrayed me. To forgive him would have been difficult, but what he asks now seems impossible.

"I am leaving next week for Croatia. I won't be back for some months. Tell me you'll think on it. Please."

It's too much. He chooses to ask me now? I can't give him any promise. He must know, because he opens the door and lets me pass without another word.

Twenty-Three

Okazja na nikogo nie czeka.
Wait too long and the opportunity is sure to vanish.

Tired and broken, I sat there, listening to Franz's sermon. It was only an accident two mornings ago, but Mania's anger ran deep. One misstep—a spilled bowl of porridge. I had not been allowed to eat since.

Franz paused, his arms outstretched, and sent me a look of warning.

I straightened in an instant, rubbing my drooping eyes. I could not fall asleep again, not that day. I was much too weak for further punishment.

"The one who made all, and gives all, suffered for you," Franz said, pointing to the cross above.

Suffered for me? My life was suffering enough—Mania, Jozef, the chores. Why did God suffer, too? And how did that help me?

A single ray of sunlight emerged from the window above, its light resting on the cross. I imagined it straight from heaven, that God was somehow there, watching me and telling me there was a path just for me—a path far better than my pain, a path He would lead me to. I felt a stirring in my heart and a promise of His love.

I try to push the memory away, yet it comes back again and again.

I don't believe God makes anyone do anything. But maybe He offers a path, a light I can choose to follow.

I felt it coming to America, and I feel it now. I'm not at the mercy of a brother now. I haven't anyone to claim me or tell me what I must do. I breathe easier at night now, and I wake knowing I'll decide, in large part, what each new day will bring.

Mike comes to my mind, but he's far from my reach now. He spoke about my freedom, but it's difficult to trust any man. Would he become my ruler like so many men have tried to be?

My father abandoned me; Jozef neglected and worked me; Franz preached to me; Vic used me; Marco wanted me. I lie in bed at night, contemplating these men. Sometimes I cry, and other times I scream into my pillow.

Without fail, my mind wanders back to Oliwjer, Andrzejek, Petar, Igor. Were they better men, or did I just imagine them to be?

I still see Marco—before work, after work, each time I pass Turnbol's. He doesn't speak to me anymore, not after what happened. He gives a sad smile, a faint wave of his hand, or just a swift glance. In time, he'll no longer see me, and I hope it's sooner rather than later.

"Be brave, Stella. Time heals all wounds," Tia continues to tells me.

I smile in response each time, but my heart is heavy and weary. So often I feel nothing at all.

The doll is soft in my hands, and I run my fingers over each stitch. It was sewn with such care. The hair is made of dark yarn, fastened into braids. The dress is white cotton, pressed and hemmed. Dabs of pink mark the cheeks, two buttons as the eyes.

"Oh, it's lovely, Stella," Tia says, leaning closer.

I smile, nodding. "It reminds me of Bronia." I turn to the woman at the booth. "How much?" I ask.

"Fifty cents."

My cheeks flush, and I look to my purse: only forty.

Tia clasps my hand. "Fifty? I wouldn't pay more than thirty."

The woman cringes.

"Let's go," Tia says, nudging me.

Running my fingers along the fabric, I sigh. Bronia never owned anything so beautiful. She would cherish it. I can almost see her, snuggling close to me, doll in arm, listening to my stories.

I smile, recalling my story of the black birch branches. I can hear her mixture of Croatian and Polish, even now. Her dark eyes come to me, even though the rest of her face has faded. I long to hold her in my arms again, to hear her whisper, "Ciocia Stella." But she has grown stronger and older while I've been away, the memory of me less sweet, less frequent.

"Forty cents is all I have," I say, without looking up.

"Forty cents?" The woman asks, shuffling closer. She takes the doll, examining it. "Forty cents it is."

Tia winces as I empty my purse. "Stella, your dinner."

I shrug. "Will you help me write to her?"

She smiles, her eyes glistening. "Yes, if that's what you wish."

I make the note short. *My love for you is evergreen. Do not forget me.*

We wrap the gift, along with the note, into a brown bundle. I keep it in my bag until I can earn the postage, until I gain the courage to send it. At least, that's what I tell myself.

If I send the doll to Bronia, it will mean that I haven't forgotten, that I haven't moved on. For with the good of Bronia comes the memories of Jozef and Mania, Franz, and my parents. It's impossible to pick through the memories, impossible to choose which to keep. If I send the package, I'm choosing to hold on to a piece, perhaps more than I want to. So, the package sits in my bag and waits, and with it, I carry the weight of my past.

"Will you come dancing with me?" Tia asks, brushing her long dark hair.

"Not tonight," I say, staring at the wall behind her.

"You haven't gone in over two months. Why not?" she asks, crinkling her brows.

"I can't do it, not yet."

A knock at the door sounds, and Tia rises from her chair. She cracks the door, and she lowers her voice. "You wish to speak to Stella?"

Then I hear it, that old familiar voice—Vic.

I startle, collecting myself, praying for composure.

He waits for me at the door. "Stella, I know you don't want to see me, but I had to come. I've a letter for you from Durliosy." His hat is lowered behind his back, his hair dripping from the recent rain.

I nod, taking the letter. "Thank you," is all I can manage.

There was something more I should have said. I am sure of it. I felt it, but Vic nods. I shut the door.

Tia casts a quick glance, her lip quivering. "Thank you?"

I lift my hand, warning her to say no more.

She returns to her chair, surrendering. "Well, Stella, who is it from?"

I shrug, curiosity replacing my distress upon seeing Vic.

Tia steps closer. "Give it here. I'll have to read it to you anyways." She pulls apart the paper, scanning it. Her eyes meet mine, confusion flashing across her face. "Who is Andrze?"

"Andrze is my childhood friend. Why? Has he written?" I lean closer. "Tia, what does he say?"

Her lips part, a sigh escaping. "Alright, alright." She clears her throat. "'Stella. So much has happened since you left to America. The pain of our goodbye lingered in my heart, but it is now replaced by an even greater loss, a greater hole.

"'Shortly after you left, I married Lodzia. Oliwjer grew sick, and before long, Lodzia nursed him each day, while I prepared the land. Oliwjer never recovered. My brother died, and I wished you were here to comfort me.

"No more than two days passed before Lodzia caught ill and fell to her own grave. There was nothing I could do. Lodzia and Oliwjer are gone forever, and my heart is broken.

"'I cannot stay here. I board for America in three weeks, where I hope we can be reunited once more as the dearest of friends. Andrze.'"

For a moment, the numbness is gone. I fall into Tia's arms, struggling to catch my breath. The pain and tears come as a relief. There is still a little of me left, a little more to feel, a little left to fight.

"Tia," I say between sobs. "Why is it that even the good aren't spared from the wretchedness of life?"

She trembles, pulling me a small distance away. "Stella, no one is spared from the bad or the good. We must have it all."

I fall back into her embrace.

I tell her of Andrze. It feels strange to speak of him now after so much time has passed. She only listens, asks a few questions, and shakes her head.

"Stella, what are you going to say to him?" she asks. "Do you still love him?"

I never said I loved him, but Tia must have seen it in my expression, in my eyes. I swallow, choosing my words carefully. "I don't know what I'll say, but it's Andrze. I'm not worried. He's my friend."

Tia stares at the postage, and her shoulders stiffen. "He sent this almost a month ago. It won't be long until he's here."

Twenty-Four

Łatwo przyszło, łatwo poszło.
Easy come, easy go.

Twelve days later, Andrze arrives at my door, and I'm no more prepared than if no letter had been sent at all. He's just how I remembered him—short and strong, piercing blue eyes, a big smile.

Yet he is different, too. There is sorrow behind his eyes, a familiar hint of weariness.

He hugs me, and my feet lift off the ground.

"Stella," Andrze says, setting me down. "It feels like it has been years."

"Only seven months," I say, smiling, "though it feels longer."

"You have changed," he says, tilting his head to the side.

"As have you."

We go to a café, the same one I used to meet Vic at each Saturday. Andrze struggles to focus. I can tell he isn't recovered from his travels or his sorrows.

So, we sip our soup quietly, every now and then offering some small talk. I long to ask him about Durliosy, Amalia, Bronia, or even Franz, but I worry it will pain him.

"Tell me about America, Stella. Has it been everything you wish it to be?"

I smile, hesitant. "It was good at first, finally making it off of the boat and into the country. I found work in a factory sewing clothes. It's hard work, but it's nothing to what I used to do."

Andrze swallows. "You mean they don't work you like Jozef did."

I nod. "Well, it's more difficult in some ways—the same, day in and day out. It's a different kind of tiring, like I'll never finish sewing clothes until the day I die."

He listens closely, his palms against his cheek, just as he used to sit.

"I miss the challenges of the farm, but I don't miss taking orders from my brother. I like to say that the factory is hard, but it is my choice, and that makes all the difference. So I make my way, and that is all I can hope for."

He leans closer. "And you had a falling out with Wiktor."

My mouth drops, and I gasp. "How did you—"

"It is alright, Stella. I saw it in his face when he spoke of you, when he directed me to your boardinghouse. Now, what has happened to make you both at odds?"

I wipe my hands on the napkin in my lap, staring at my feet beneath the table. "Vic is different now. He's changed. He drinks too much, and he gambles." I hear my voice tremble. I catch my breath.

Andrze stares, waiting.

"He gambled me, Andzre. He bet me in one of his games."

His jaw clenches. "What do you mean? How could he bet you?"

"It started out that he would bet my money. He came to my boardinghouse drunk one night. We quarreled about it, but he promised never to do it again." I shrug, as if it's not anything worth remembering, but Andzre can see it was bad.

"And did he keep that promise?"

My eyes fall to the floor. "He lost everything one night. He had bet everything. One of Vic's gambling friends—Marco—saw it. Marco admired me, but I'd discouraged him. So, when Marco saw Vic down on his luck, he placed a bet. If Vic won, his debt would be forgiven, but if Marco won, he would have my hand in marriage."

Andrze stands, knocking the small chair to the floor. For a moment, all the eyes of the café are on us, but he doesn't notice. "Stella, how could he?"

I place my hand across the table, reaching for his, trying to remind him of where we are.

His knitted brows fall, and he bends to pick up the chair. "So, Wiktor won then. At least you are safe, but he should never have made such a bet."

I shake my head, offering a sad smile. "No, Andrze. Vic didn't win, but neither did Marco. Marco's brother caught ear of it, and he won. Mike won't make me marry him, but he said I deserved a hand for my freedom." I look down once more, irritated. "Mike has gone back to Croatia to see his family, and I'm safe from it all. Now you see why I can't ever go back to Vic. He used me worse than Jozef ever did."

Andrze bites the inside of his lip. "It angers me your brothers treat you ill. Where is Stanislaus? Does he not have any pride to save his sister?"

I almost choke on my soup. "Oh, no. Stan doesn't live in Fells Point. He left Vic last year. I haven't seen him. He doesn't even know I'm here."

"So you still have no one to look out for you," Andzre says, raking a hand through his hair.

I drop my spoon, the tinkling sound catching my friend's gaze once more. "I look out for myself now. I'm independent, no one to answer to and no one to ask. And I've a friend, Tia. She treats me better than my family ever did. She—"

"But it is still not what you deserve, Stella," he says, interrupting me.

What I deserve? It's been so long since I've heard that word, but it still bothers me. I feel it. There's a distance between Andzre and me that was never there before.

"Andrze, I will be alright. What about you? Tell me about your letter. You must still be carrying the heartache of losing Lodzia and Oliwjer."

Andrze's eyes gloss over, and his bottom lip trembles. I think he might cry, but he only closes his eyes, exhaling. "Oh, Stella. It is more than heartache. Oliwjer, then her. She was . . . she was so sick. We had only been married five months, but it felt like an eternity. She was an angel, and it pains me to speak of her, but you must know: When she left this earth, she took another with her."

"Then she was with child?"

Andrze nods, wiping a lone tear.

Tears trickle down my own cheek. To lose a wife and a child in the same breath? It's more sorrow than anyone should have to carry. "Andrze," I say, between gasps, "I'm so sorry."

He dries his eyes, avoiding my gaze. "It is my reality. You don't need to say anything, but I thought you should know." He stops, his eyes lighting. "Your brother Franz told me they are in heaven and that I must live so that I may join them. He also said I might contemplate coming to church more frequently."

I laugh, shaking my head. "That's what Franz would think of. I'm sorry he's like that."

Andrze smiles, rolling his eyes. "I suppose he meant well."

"Will you tell me what happened when I left?" I ask, changing the subject.

He nods. "As you expect, Mania and Jozef were angry, especially Mania. But she improves, and she is learning to do more. Perhaps she didn't realize what she was capable of until she had to do things on her own."

"I'm glad to hear that. And what of Bronia? Is she upset at me for abandoning her?" I ask, unsure if I even want to know his answer.

"Oh, Stella," he says, brushing his hand over mine. "Bronia would never be angry at you. Yes, she was sad for many months. She is still sad, but she is learning to get along without you, as is everyone."

My eyes pool. "Does she speak of me?"

Andzre smiles. "Yes, she speaks of you often, at least when I see her. She told me of the birch branches." He pauses, locking eyes with me. "They meant everything to her."

My heart swells, a weight lifted. If what he says is true, then she understood.

"Your brothers were upset with me," he says. "Franz only let me come to the church because it was his religious duty. It was not until my wedding that his anger faded. And after Oliwjer's and Lodzia's passings, Franz took it upon himself to visit me daily. It was actually his idea that I come to America."

"And Amalia?"

He swallows, hesitating. "She thought it was selfish of you," he says, shaking his head.

I nod. I knew not everyone would understand why I left. Sometimes I'm not even certain. I dab my sleeve at my eyes. "Andzre, what will you do? Where will you work now that you are here?"

He sighs, lifting his arms in the air. "Your brother says there is work at the meat packing plant."

"It isn't a set job. Vic doesn't get work every day, and he goes without meals. I believe it's what drove him to gamble and drink."

"I am not your brother. Don't worry, Stella. When I constructed the new house for Lodzia, I realized I am good with my hands, that I might make a living of it. Baltimore needs builders like me, but I will have to learn some English first, or at least find work with those that do. In the meantime, I'll go to the meat packing plant."

"I'm sure you're right," I say, smiling.

A change has taken place, for being here, with Andrze beside me, I no longer feel heartache, only friendship and sisterly love. And, what's more alarming, is that after he leaves and I walk back to the boardinghouse, it's Mike who comes to my mind.

After my fight with Vic, I was so angry with Mike. I yelled and accused him. But Mike understood; he was kind.

Mike has always seen a part of me that others didn't. And, if I'm honest with myself, I understand him, too. He isn't as compassionate and understanding as Andrze, and he would never marry me just to take care of me as Andrze once offered.

Mike is a different kind of good man.

I shut the thoughts off, knowing I'll lose my wits if I don't.

This will pass. I'm barely a girl. I don't wish to marry yet.

Twenty-Five

Więcej słuchaj, a mniej mów - zawsze szkodzi zbytek słów.
Keep your mouth shut and ears open.

Tia and I work in unison, passing each other the spools and needles, scissors, and scrap bin.

The women at the station are quiet, the machines from clear across the different floors humming, a dissonant and eerie melody. The clipping of horses and the dinging of the trolleys sound below, and the rhythmic sounds remind me of a dreary song my father used to sing about the Russian soldiers.

Mr. Pruski is out of his wits today. The owners of the factory will be here tomorrow to take their children on a tour. Mr. Pruski is making sure the stations are in order.

"Do you think Mr. Jackson's children will like the factory?" Clara, a new member of our station asks.

Lucy shrugs. "It must be exciting for the children to see what real work is,"

Tia gives a faint smile. "Yes. This is what will get you ten dollars a week."

That's when I notice the faint echoing of men, clamoring and running from beneath. I rise to the doorway, then the stairwell, listening for more.

"Fire!" a woman screams, sobbing from a floor below.

The word spreads like the fire itself—catching from ear to mouth, until everyone is frenzied, sprinting toward the stairs.

We reach the stairwell, and already there's a haze, thick and gray smoke billowing up. The doors are locked, and no one can get out.

I cover my mouth, coughing against my shoulder. The heat rises with the smoke, and my face drips in sweat. It's spreading, and fast.

"Stella, what are we going to do? All these girls—how will we get out?" Tia's green eyes are widened, her expression pale and panic-stricken.

This can't be the end. It isn't right.

Women are coughing, crying, and convulsing. A few slink down the edge of the wall, as if they have given up.

A woman behind me smashes the window and jumps out. I see her pass to the pavement.

"Tia," I say, "Maybe we should climb down a window."

I make the mistake of glancing out the nearest window, horrified to see the result of the woman's jump. Her body lies on the pavement, broken and bloodied.

She's dead. And she isn't the only one.

I gasp, swallowing the bile climbing my throat. I pull the scarf from around my neck and cover my mouth.

"Cover you face, Tia," I say.

She follows suit, and we push our way through, scrambling up the third floor. The elevator shaft catches my eyes. It's open, a few boxes loaded to the side.

"Tia! The elevator."

We both run, a line of women trailing us. We pack in the old metal box, shutting the mesh door and the outer shell.

"Does anyone know how to operate this?" I ask.

They shake their head, some shrugging. There is blankness in their gazes, a panic in their open mouths.

I've seen it done enough, and with no time for hesitation, we begin our descent. It takes Tia and me working together to pull the break at the bottom floor. We pull the doors open, running to safety.

The police have already blocked off the street, and the stairwell opens. Women flood from the doors, trampling one another.

"Tia," I say. "I can't stay a moment longer."

But Tia isn't listening. She's fixed on the images—the women lying in the street, the woman being treated for horrific burns. They're unconscious, if not dead.

I stagger forward, grasping at a lantern pole to keep from falling. I want to tell Tia to look away, but I can't. I can't look away.

Tia sobs, shaking all over.

"Tia!" I say, finally getting her attention. "Let's go home."

Twenty-Six

Kto nie idzie naprzód, ten się cofa.
He who does not advance goes backward.

Only five dead. That's what everyone is saying. Only five dead. They say this like it's something to be celebrated. But I saw the bodies of those that jumped. I saw the burned.

Five lives lost: four women, one man. There isn't anything to celebrate.

Women were trapped on the stairwells, many of them sick from the smoke. It's possible even more will die.

The factory was ordered to give each worker two weeks' pay, and work on the upper floors will resume within the month.

I cringe when I think of returning to that locked cage.

"You are quiet, Stella," Andrze says, sipping his coffee.

The café is less busy than usual, the empty chairs and tables beside me a welcome sight. "Is there something you want to talk about?" I ask.

He shrugs. "Are you going to be alright here?" he asks.

"I'll be fine." I clear my throat, nodding. "The fire has given me time to think. There's so much more I want from life. I'll make it here in America. I'm happy."

"Are you?" he asks, skepticism etching into the wrinkles near his eyes.

"You think I was happier in Durliosy?" I ask, folding my arms.

"I know you were mistreated by your family. You felt pain. It's just that you also felt other things there—things you don't seem to remember. You were happy with Bronia, around my brother and me. But now, you are so alone—"

I raise my hand to stop him. "But I'm not alone. I have you and Tia."

He clicks his tongue, shaking his head. "And yet you seem more alone than ever. You are determined not to need anyone or anything. Some would call it being stubbornly independent."

I push my mug to the edge of the table. "And what would you call it?" I ask, irritation coating each word.

He shrugs once more. "Loneliness?" He straightens, reaching his hand toward me. "Stella, I am proud of you. You have done so much."

"But?" I ask, hearing the hesitation in his voice.

"But I just want you to be happy. It is not enough merely to survive another day."

There's a connection between those that suffer. We all feel it—me, Tia, and Andrze. The journey on the boat was only the beginning. We used to think it was the hardest part; we were wrong.

Perhaps the mountains are the easiest to summit, the hills the hardest to overcome. For these bumps are ongoing, all day and every day. There's no end to the challenges of life.

Andrze sighs. "I say this as your friend, Stella. There is something out there greater than a week's wages and a warm bed. The future can be full of companionship and promise." He pauses, trying to overcome the emotion that has clearly overwhelmed him. He hangs his head, a few tears rolling down the side of his cheek. "I say this because I know this. Lodzia brought me so much happiness. My future was with her and the baby. Now that she is gone, I know I must find a new future."

I've never entrusted my happiness to another person, but then again, I've not felt the joy he speaks of. "Andrze, Andrze," I say, squeezing his hand. "You'll find your future here. You'll be happy again."

He pulls away, wiping at his eyes and tossing his hair backward. "I hope, but it will not be here. I am leaving for Chicago this week."

"Chicago?" I ask.

"Yes. There is a large settlement of Poles there. I will have better luck finding work building."

I swallow, speechless again. He's leaving me—another goodbye.

"Stella, I hoped I could be your happiness, just as I hoped before you left Durliosy, but it won't do. We are like brother and sister."

I nod. I knew Andrze wouldn't stay forever. Not then, and not now. But still, it aches to hear he is leaving. "You will write me from Chicago?" I ask. "Go where you need to go, but know that I'll miss you."

He smiles. "I have always cared about you as much as if you were my own blood."

Then he hugs me and walks me back to my boardinghouse.

In a matter of minutes, I lie on my bed, shaking as I sob. I feel the pain he spoke of. I feel everything at once, and I realize I've been deceiving myself.

I'm not happy.

And now Andrze is gone. I cry. I don't feel the heartache for him that I once did, but I feel the ache of losing myself. He's always been a part of me—at first my dearest friend, then a part of my past when I left Durliosy. He's no longer part of that past; yet he's not a part of my future either.

I turn all night, barely closing my eyes.

I recall the sting of Mania's slaps, Bronia's arms around my neck, Franz's exaggerated sermons and censures. I ache at the thought of pulling the cart, the worry of my future, the heartache of a first love, and the uncertainty of my future. The pain courses through me, encircling my heart and escaping with my tears.

And though I am sick with emotion, though the weight threatens to crush me, I relive it once more. There are parts of my past that can't be closeted. For if I do, I'll lose myself.

Andrze is right. I need my past to find happiness in my future. I can't begin without collecting the pieces—the parts of me that I've tried so hard to abandon.

Twenty-Seven

Nie wszystko złoto, co się świeci.

All that glitters is not gold.

"Marzewska," Mr. Pruski calls, beckoning me to follow.

"Evaluations," Lucy says, pursing her lips. "Good luck, Stella."

I've been distracted, and I try to prepare for his scolding. I returned to the factory two weeks ago, but something has changed, and I can't stay. It's as if my entire life of struggle plays on my mind each time I step inside. I feel compelled to keep moving forward, and yet each time I enter the building, it feels like a step backward.

"Miss Marzewska, do you enjoy your work here?" he asks. He repositions his belt, and the keys in his pocket jingle. "Are you happy here?"

I don't know how to respond to such a question. No one enjoys their work here. It's the eating and surviving that induces me to keep such hours and endure the monotony.

"You're one of my best workers, despite your distractedness. I shouldn't be encouraging you to leave—"

"Leave?" I lurch forward. "Have I done something wrong?"

He shakes his head. "You see, my sister has a small laundering service on Thames Street. She's looking for a new girl to work for her. I can't promise you'd love it, but it's better pay and fewer hours." He pauses, gesturing toward the factory floor. "And you would be out of this insufferable building. I've given her your name, should you wish to accept the position. She provides room and board."

Tears threaten to prick my eyes, but I smile, choking back the emotion. "I'd be more than happy to assist your sister, Mr. Pruski. Thank you."

He smiles at me. It's the only time I've seen him smile. "She'll be happy to have you. Come by my office after your shift, and I'll give you more instructions and your week's pay."

I return to my station in a daze of gratitude and confusion. I'm reminded of the wool the old merchant gifted me at market. I had only wished it, and once again, I know God has heard my wish, the aching of a life worth living.

"Well, how did it go?" Tia asks.

"Well."

Lucy puffs. "Well? Evaluations with Pruski never go well. What happened?"

I shake my head, not wanting to cause trouble for Mr. Pruski or the other girls. "He noticed I'm distracted, but says I'm a good worker."

Lucy raises one brow, looking to Tia. "That's a first."

Tia smiles, ignoring Lucy. "I'm glad to hear it."

It isn't until after our shift and the walk home that I tell Tia.

"You'll be out of the factory then?" she asks. "And the boardinghouse?"

I hesitate, not wanting to upset her. "I'll still see you."

She surprises me by throwing her arms around my neck. "Oh, Stella. I'm so happy for you."

With muffled sobs and a tight embrace, we celebrate.

I carry the basket of clothes to the roof and hang them to dry. I relish in the cool breeze. The far-off trees are beginning to change color. The oranges and golds are much more beautiful to me than the greens ever were. They feel so warm, so comforting, and I secretly wish for a country home and a family of my own to tend.

I chide myself. Maybe, like the trees, I'm changing. Perhaps these desires aren't as far from my grasp as they once were. Perhaps, I've gained a new dream, a new path to follow.

Valeria's shop isn't large, but it's comfortable. Without the humming of the machines and the scolding of the managers, I'm content.

Behind the shop showroom are the lodging quarters. There are three boarding rooms in total and seven girls. We share a bathroom. It's temporary for most of us, all except Valeria and her daughter, Ana.

"Stella," Ana says, climbing the steps. She's only eleven, but she helps with the business each day after school.

"Yes?" I toss my last garment on the line, pinning it, before turning toward her.

"Tia's downstairs," Ana says.

I gather the basket, giving one last glance to the view behind me before descending the stairs. "I'm coming."

I usually visit Tia on her days off. The factory life weighs on her much more than it used to. She says it's because I'm no longer there beside her. I believe it's something more. She needs a change.

"You came," I say, hugging her.

"I thought it only fair. You visit me most of the time." Her eyelids are heavy, and the bags beneath have grown since the last time I saw her. "Are you done with work yet?"

I nod. "How are you?"

She cranes her neck, raising a brow. "Tired."

"Cheer up," I say, untying my apron. "It's your day off tomorrow. Let's get dinner."

Tia chuckles, placing her hands on her hips. "Honestly, Stella, are you telling me to cheer up as I used to tell you?"

"Maybe," I say, surprised to hear my own laughter.

She puts an arm around me. "Maybe we should go dancing tonight then."

It's been months since we went with Marco and Mike.

I shake my head. I'm not ready for that.

"No, no, Stella," she explains, "I know another place where many of the Poles and Slavs gather. You won't see the Nosic brothers there. I've already gone once without you. It's a good crowd."

I nod, surprised at how quick I was to worry. Mike is in Croatia now, perhaps forever, and I could do with a little happiness and life as Andzre suggested.

"Only if you will fix my hair," I say.

Tia laughs again. "I've been waiting for you to ask."

"Tia," I say, when she combs my hair into a bun. "Will your father ever remarry? He's still young, and there are more than enough women who would be willing."

She shrugs. "I don't ask these things. Matka was so sick, and my father mourned her loss for so long. I don't think he's recovered, but I see some improvements. He smiles more, and he laughs again. Someday he won't need me anymore."

I grasp her hand against my neck. "Tia, how can you say that? Your father will always need you. You're his strength."

She breaks her hand away, grabbing the hair that I've sent falling down my back. "Of course we are close, closer than most daughters and fathers. It's because he has needed me so badly that I haven't tried to marry yet. He needs someone to take care of him."

I nod. "But you wish to marry?"

Tia sighs. "Oh, Stella, of course I do. I long for that kind of love, for a family of my own."

She finishes the last of my hair, pinning it along the crown and putting my mother's hairpin into the back of her creation. She sighs. "Perfect."

Then I ask what I've feared for so long. "Do you think I'm strange because I don't welcome the attention of men?"

She smiles, resting her light eyes on me. "I think you're beautiful, Stella."

I wait, hoping she'll find the strength to answer. For some people, honesty is difficult.

"Stella, you are strange, but not in the way you suppose. I can see you have been hurt many times. Your father, your brothers, Marco. I can't blame you for your desire to stay away from men. It's just that

I think you'll miss happiness if you stay this way. You didn't see the love my father had for my mother, the love my grandparents shared. You've only seen marriages built on a mutual need to survive. There are better kinds of love."

I twist my fingers around my skirt, biting the inside of my cheek. "Do you really think there is more to it than that?"

Tia's expression changes. "Of course there is, and you know it, Stella. I saw the way you looked at Mike."

My jaw drops. "Mike? What are you talking about?"

She laughs. "There was something between the pair of you. In any case, let's go dancing."

She reaches for the door handle, but I stop her, placing my hand on her shoulder. "You think I found happiness in Mike?"

Tia shrugs. "I think you could've found something like that with Mike."

"Well, he's gone now," I say, surprising myself.

She faces me, pulling me into an embrace. "Oh, Stella. We both need to dance. Let's go."

I follow her out the door, but my thoughts stay with Mike. I don't know why I waited so long to admit my affections, but the pain that creeps into my heart tells me it was more than friendship.

Something changed in between everything else—the struggles with Vic, the strain of the factory work, the newness of this country. Feelings for Mike made their way to my heart. And yet he has been gone for months, and he may never come back to me—not after the fight with Marco, not after my seeming indifference to his proposal.

So, like the time I left Andrze at the train station in Ostroleka, heartbroken but determined, I will move on once more and hope that I find my way.

Twenty-Eight

Fall 1908

Nie pytaj starego, pytaj bywałego.
Do not ask the old—ask the experienced.

It's been almost two years since I arrived in Fells Point, the seasons flowing as quickly as the days. And yet time has changed and challenged everything I am and was.

Already I am forgetting Durliosy, whether I want to or not. Not everything has faded, but much of the uncertainty and pain has. I sent the package to Bronia just yesterday. It isn't so hard to think about it now—my past—and sometimes I find my mind wandering to a cold night, gathered around the old table, silently hoping Jozef will hear my plea to go to America.

I smile, recollecting how it happened, how far I am from what I was and where I was. But life is still about surviving from one day to the next. I have no cart to weigh me down, but there are new weights—perhaps stronger—strapped around my ankles, strapped around my heart.

After the new year, Valeria lost work to another laundry business and needed to economize. She let three of the girls go in order to cut prices.

Ana is twelve now. She quit school this year to help with the laundering. The workload is much heavier without the other girls. I remind myself of where I've been—it's nothing to the factory, nothing to Vic's gambling, and most certainly nothing to Mania. Yet it's a race, a race that never ends. From dawn until supper is work, and even then, there's more.

There are so many like me in the city. We come from different backgrounds. Some have been here longer, while others are new. We come broken, hoping for healing.

And it does come in sorts, but not the way I envisioned. It doesn't come at once or even very quickly. Instead, it comes with each day's rest and food, a thought of work, a belief of making it. Slowly, we see a different way, a way of happiness. It's in the faces of those I meet, the laughter of a dance, the sweetness of a child.

But then I go back to what I always do. Work. Survive. Hope.

Sometimes the hope is hard, but the work and surviving aren't possible without it. Hope is what keeps me hanging on each day. There are those that lose it—the women and men who jump the docks, the children who roam the streets in tears. I can't let myself become one of them, not after the journey I've already made.

So today I choose to wash, to hang, to iron, to fold. It's become so mechanical, as if I'm one of the machines in the factory or the wheels on the train against the track.

Ana watches me with awe. "Stella, what do you think of when you work?" she asks.

I shrug. "Everything really. I work quickly with my hands, but my mind moves at a much slower pace. I think about many things—the weather, Tia, my brother, where I came from, and anything else that comes to me."

Ana smiles. "And the stories?"

I flash her a knowing look. I've only recently begun to tell her my stories. She's much too old for most of them, but she listens still the same.

"Always my stories," I say, grinning.

It's true. The stories have come back. Valeria asks I speak in Polish because she worries Ana will lose her native tongue. I used to tell Bronia the stories in Polish, too, even though Mania spoke

Croatian. I wanted to keep the stories as my own, and now I share them with Ana, once more in Polish.

"Will you help me with my deliveries, Stella?" Ana asks.

I smile back. "Of course."

We spend the next hour packaging the laundry in parcels, one for each address on our delivery route.

Ana write the names. I can't write well, but I know the streets, and I remember each house and name on the list. The route is so familiar now, and I could do it in my sleep, as the Americans say.

We travel the streets with our carts.

"I'll take this one," Ana says, pointing toward the door of the first customer on our list.

I stay with the cart, watching her braids bounce in sync with her steps. She knocks, hands the package to a woman and returns to my side.

"First one done," Ana says, glancing past me. Her eyes brighten, and she waves to someone across the street.

I turn, smiling when I see Mr. Gerbat, a friend of Valeria. "Mr. Gerbat," I say, waving.

He crosses the street. "Hello, Stella, Miss Ana. Off to deliveries today?" He strokes his graying mustache. "And how is your mother, Ana?"

"Busy as always, Sir."

"Yes, bless her soul, always working so hard. You're lucky to have her, the both of you."

Ana perks up. "Will you be stopping by later after work, Mr. Gerbat?"

He shakes his head. "Your mother might need a break after such a long day. But if she were to invite me herself, I might find it acceptable." He pulls at his suspenders, and I can see the thought of Valeria makes him nervous.

"Please come," I say, placing my hand on his arm. "We always enjoy your company. Perhaps we can persuade Valeria to go dancing?"

Mr. Gerbat blushes, shuffling from side to side. He mumbles something about how rain is on its way and he must be going, though there aren't any clouds in the sky. Still flushed, he tips his cap. "I really must be going," he says.

"Goodbye," Ana says.

I lift my hand to wave, but something from behind Mr. Gerbat catches my eye.

I blink in disbelief, my voice choking in my throat. There, leaning against a lamp post, stands a tall, dark figure. His features are almost indistinguishable in the shadow and between the passing carriages, but I recognize his posture and outline in an instance.

I stand motionless, my heart racing, my pulse hot against my skin.

"Stella?" Ana asks. "Are you alright? You look like you've seen a ghost."

I force a small laugh, shaking my head quickly. "I thought I saw someone I once knew."

I look back, but the man is gone.

Ana has already pulled her cart up the broken path, and so I grab mine, walking to catch her.

"Do you think Mr. Gerbat will really come to the shop tonight?" Ana asks.

"Maybe. It's clear he wishes to know your mother better. Do you think she'd like it?" I ask, still trying to calm my racing heart.

Ana shrugs. "I think Matka has been alone a long time. Mr. Gerbat is kind."

"And you? What do you think of it all?"

Ana smiles. "I think that she should marry him. It's hard to be a widow in this city. Matka has done well enough considering, but it would be good for us. Marriage is important. She tells me so herself."

I nod. "So I hear, but is Mr. Gerbat the man you wish her to marry?"

She laughs. "Why should it matter who she marries, as long as he's kind and doesn't drink too much? Mr. Gerbat has a job and treats us well."

Ana keeps talking, but I hardly notice. Maybe it's my reminiscing that distracts me. I can't seem to wrap my mind around what I saw today, who I saw.

Tia shifts her weight. "I saw Vic a few days ago. He got married last month to Alice and is moving to Chicago to look for work. He leaves on the train tomorrow. That's what he says anyways. Have you spoken to him?"

My palms are hot against my cheek. "You know I haven't seen him since he brought Andzre's letter."

Tia nods, but her expression is disapproving.

"And you think I should see him?" I ask. "I'm not going to. I wish him well wherever he goes, but I can't talk to him after what happened. He chose his own neck over mine, and that isn't the way of family."

Tia gives a sad smile, a small line tracing her lips on one side. "I just thought you should know."

"I can't always be the sister when there's not a brother to act the part," I say, satisfied with my rationale.

Tia winces. "But aren't you doing the same as he did, choosing your own neck over his?"

My anger flares, and the words come too quickly. "He chose this, Tia—not me—when he bet my entire future in a game of cards to save his own skin. He made this choice, and he must live with it as I do."

I haven't forgotten my brother; I think of him often. He helped me to get to America. I feel indebted, and if it weren't for his drinking and gambling, he would have been an honorable brother. But his habits ruled him, and he was too risky and thoughtless when he was under the influence of alcohol and desperation.

Thoughts of him lead to feelings of betrayal, anger, and even loathing; they flare in my chest like a wildfire. I try to recall the good moments too, and gratitude and fondness inch their way beside the anger in my heart.

Yet they slip away, melting into only sadness.

"So you're done with him. But don't you think it would put your mind at rest, seeing him once more before he goes, parting on better terms?" Her eyes fill with concern.

Tia doesn't give up easily, but I'm not interested in speaking about it further. I smile and place my hand on her shoulder. "You're a good friend, Tia. I will think on it."

Twenty-Nine

Gwiazdki z nieba się zachciewa.
There is no building bridges across the ocean.

I never could say anything to Vic. I walked two miles to Camden Station yesterday. The clouds overhead turned gray, a drizzle by the time I made it. The grand architecture—the molding along the ceilings, the wide pillars, and the chandeliers—overwhelmed my senses.

Memories raced across my mind—Vic's letter with my passage, a shared dance after arriving, his drunken rage, his sobbing tears. The memories race, the good colliding with the bad, until I no longer can separate them. I wanted to go to him, yet the pain and uncertainty held me back.

But I went.

I stood behind a pillar, dodging the sight of the passengers as they came and went. It wasn't hard to spot Vic. His worn cap and dirty trousers, his broad shoulders and easy smile—he entered the station with Alice in tow, a shared suitcase between the pair.

Alice smiled when Vic took the case from her, guiding her to a bench opposite me. He leaned and kissed her cheek, then left to purchase tickets.

Her cheeks pinked at his touch, her warm gaze trailing his every movement. She sat straight, her light hair braided into a twist at the crown of her head.

Do you know about his gambling, his drinking? I wanted to ask.

Vic returned from the counter, taking her hand in his own.

I only watched, reluctant to confront him. I've never reveled in goodbyes.

When the bell sounded, Vic helped his wife up the steps, dropping the suitcase near the track. He returned for it, nearly stumbling when he caught sight of me.

We locked eyes for mere moments.

Neither of us smiled, waved. There was no greeting, and no goodbye.

Yet there was an understanding of sorts—shared sorrow and regret, a trace of gratitude, a portion of forgiveness, and, perhaps, well wishes. Can such things be exchanged without a word? Most would argue no, but I believe we did. Maybe it wasn't what Tia wanted, or even what it should have been, but it was what I could give, and it was better than not going at all.

My stroll down East Pratt Street—the misty rain and muddy walks, the trolley dings and carriage wheels—does little to erase the confusion of the morning. I return to Fells Point in a daze, unable to pull myself from distraction and the maze of memories.

At first, I believe his figure an imagination, the effect of my muddled mind and the draining morning. I keep walking. He smiles and speaks my name, but I keep walking still. But then he takes my hand and pulls me to a halt, and I know it isn't a dream.

Mike Nosic has come back.

"Stella," he says, tipping his cap.

His brown eyes search my own, and I swallow hard, attempting a smile. My heart races, the shock pulsing through my veins.

"So, you do recognize me?" he asks.

My cheeks burn, remembering our last meeting and the many times since that I have thought of him, hoping he would come back. "Of course," I say. "You're back?"

Mike grins, pushing his hands into his pockets. "Yes, I've been hoping I would see you again. Are you alright? Has something happened?"

I shake my head, smiling. "I'm only late getting to work."

"You must be getting back then. Can we talk another time?" he asks.

"Yes, another time," I say, blushing at the eagerness that pours from each word.

His eyes flicker across my cheeks, his grin rising once more. "Where can I find you?"

"The laundry shop on Thames," I say, pointing at the row of businesses.

"Thames Street. I'll come soon."

After he leaves, I feel it again—that feeling that left me so hopeful in Durliosy. Just as I can't recall Vic without the accompanying grief, I can't look to Mike without hope.

I've tried envisioning my life without Mike, my life alone. There will come a time when I'll have to choose—to let him back into my heart, or turn him away for good.

Change is coming, maybe even blowing in with the wind.

The door swings shut, the bell tinkling against the glass and rousing me from my work.

"One moment," I say, tying the twine in a bow—the last of my deliveries wrapped.

"It's only me," Tia says, meeting me at the counter. "I've brought you a gift."

"Tia," I say, rising to meet her. "You didn't need to."

"Your birthday," she says, staggering forward. "And besides, there's something I've been wanting to talk to you about."

I startle, nearly dropping the bundle in my arms—Tia's usual olive complexion has paled, her green eyes misty with tears.

"Tia?" I ask, tilting my head to the side. "What's happened?"

She bites her trembling lip, bowing her head. "I've come to say goodbye." She hands me a package, shrugging. The gift is light, wrapped in discarded paper and tied with a blue ribbon. "I didn't want to leave without giving you one last present."

"What are you talking about, Tia? What do you mean goodbye?"

She steps back, motioning for me to come no closer. "You know how the factory is, how long the hours are. My father is taking me out West, to a mining town in Winton, Wyoming. A group of Poles are going. He says we'll leave tomorrow with the group."

My stomach drops. "Why so sudden, so fast? Can't he wait to decide?" I step toward her again, this time pulling her into an embrace.

She shakes her head, burying it in my neck. "He's been considering it for some time. I should've told you, but I hoped Valeria would hire me, that our circumstances here would improve. The other men decided last week to leave tomorrow. I know how you hate goodbyes, and I didn't want to prolong it."

I swat her arm, tears prickling my eyes. "Tia, you shouldn't have."

She smiles, but tears pool around her green eyes. "I know. I'll miss you, Stella. I wish I could take you with me." She pulls back, pointing to the package. "Don't forget."

I nod, choking back sobs. "You won't reconsider staying?"

"My father needs me," she says. "And besides, I need this change."

I blink back the tears, clutching the package to my chest. "I understand; I've felt it too—the necessity of change. I won't fight you on it, no matter how badly I wish to."

She hugs me once more, kissing my cheek. "Goodbye, Stella."

I squeeze her back, reluctant to say the words.

But there is no waiting, and my friend leaves, disappearing like the seasons—fading into the distance, blowing with the wind. She did it as painlessly as she could, knowing that a long goodbye would only make it worse.

Behind the ribbon and newsprint, I find a slice of fresh potica. It's my favorite treat. Familiar, comforting, and sweet—like Tia. New tears spring, and I smile, overwhelmed by the parallel.

It's little wonder then, that when Mr. Gerbat comes calling for Valeria, I say nothing, give him not so much as a glance. It's little wonder that I miss dinner and lay on my bed.

This wind seems to have taken away so much of what I love.

"Stella," Valeria says through the door. "Are you alright?"

I ignore her, pretending I can't hear her, hoping she'll leave.

She cracks the door and rushes to my side. Her touch is cool against my forehead, her voice heavy with maternal concern. "You're ill."

"No, Valeria, not ill," I say, eyes still closed, "just tired."

She leans, and a clatter against my bedtable sounds. "Then I suppose I'll just leave these here."

I sit up, opening my eyes. The hall lantern shines across the space, lighting three water lilies afloat in a bowl.

"A visitor?" I ask.

"Yes, a Mike Nosic," Valeria says with a grin. "Very handsome man. He didn't want to disturb you, but he hoped you'd go to breakfast with him tomorrow, on your day off."

I touch my matted hair, glance across the room at my pale reflection. "Yes," I say. "Tell him tomorrow. I can't see him right now."

Valeria nods, stroking my back. "I'll tell him you're resting." She steps across the room and stops near the door. "I thought you might. It isn't every day that you see such a fine young man."

I roll to my side to keep my smile hidden. Mike Nosic brought me flowers.

Thirty

Chudoba cnoty nie traci.
Freedom's just another word for nothing left to lose.

His fork skims across the plate, scooping his last bite of breakfast sausage. "And after the fire?" Mike asks, leaning across the table.

I brush my hands, dusting off the powder sugar. "After the fire, I left the factory to work for Valeria. I couldn't stay."

"I imagine not," he says, propping an arm beneath his chin. "Pain has a tendency to propel us forward."

Mike is thinner than before, his muscular shoulders weakened from his time away from the docks. I scan his face, the stubble along his jaw and cheeks. His eyes seem sad, a dark secret hidden behind their depths. What has caused this change?

"Are you going to tell me about your time in Croatia?" I ask, nudging my second pastry toward him. "How was your mother? How long have you been back?"

Mike takes the cake, nodding. "I've only been back a month. Croatia was just how I left it. My mother—just as I left her before. She gets along well enough," he says between bites.

He clears his throat, handing the empty plate to the waitress, and takes a swig of his coffee.

"What about your father, your younger brothers? Were they glad to have you back?" I ask, urging him on.

"Your Croatian is rusty," Mike says, lifting a dark brow.

I smile. "I had no one to speak it to after you left."

"Ah," he says, inching closer. "It's good I'm back to remind you then."

"Mike," I say, sighing. "What happened when you were away?"

He shrugs, leaning back in his chair and crossing his arms. "Too much. I never should've gone back," he says, tapping his foot against the floor. "I knew the farm was in bad condition, but things were worse. My brother George died while I was away, at only seven."

"Mike," I say, hearing emotion in my own voice. "I'm sorry. No one should die that young."

"Perhaps it's better for him. This life is only pain and struggle, as they say." He shakes his head, exhaling. "If I hadn't left, maybe I could've helped him, got him better."

"You can't talk like that," I say, thinking of Bronia. It took a year for the guilt to dissipate—and even then, it was only when Andrze assured me she was well. I wouldn't wish that same guilt for Mike.

"Why not?" he asks, meeting my gaze.

"You just can't. It will only make things worse if you do."

His brown eyes are warmer than I remembered, the golden flecks like fiery torches. How could I have forgotten his eyes, his handsome jaw and angled cheeks?

I take a drink of the water, hoping it will cool my flushed face.

He chews on the inside of his cheek and raises a brow. "Not everything in life is painful." And with the slightest touch, his fingers over mine, my heart takes flight.

The connection between us is not lost.

I blush once more and clear my throat, pulling my hand away and toward my beating chest. "I thought it was your mother that was ill."

He nods. "As did I, but I found her more ill in spirits than anything. She just wanted me home. She exaggerated her condition, and she begged the little money I had off of me. She wanted me to run the farm, to forget America. I had to earn my fare back in the vineyards."

I was so consumed by the factory and sadness of Durliosy before to see beyond myself. Now I see him, perhaps in a way I never had before. "I didn't think I'd ever see you again," I say, surprising myself.

"Sorry to disappoint you," he says, grinning. "I wondered it myself when I was in Croatia. A lot can happen in a year. And when I came back, you were gone."

"I never left."

"But it was hard to find you. I almost gave up until that day in the street when I saw you delivering laundry. Your brother didn't even know where you were," he says, the hint of a question hanging between us.

I swallow. "A lot can happen in a year, but I think I'd need more time than that to reconcile myself with what he tried to do. And besides, what of your brother? You can't say you are much closer than Vic and I, can you?"

Mike laughs. "No, but I think what happened with my brother was different. He wasn't drunk like Vic was. Marco knew exactly what he was doing when he started to fight me; Vic was hardly conscious of anything but the alcohol and his own desperation. You were furthest from his thoughts." The meaning of his words flashes across his features. "I guess it wasn't any better."

"No," I say, shrugging.

He glances around the café, the midday rush just beginning. Mike puts a few coins on the table. "Let's go."

He walks me back to Thames Street, asking me more about my work with Valeria. I tell him it pays more, that my life is so much better now that I've left the factory.

"I'm glad you're happy," Mike says, standing at the door.

I smile, nodding. "And are you glad to be back?"

I wrap my scarf around my hair, avoiding his gaze. All his talk of his family left me wondering if he only came back to escape the poverty. It's one thing to look to a place with hope and another to run away. But then again, I came to America for both reasons, and maybe there are many reasons why Mike came back. Am I one of his reasons?

Mike tilts his head to the side, leaning toward me. "Glad? I'm more relieved. Going home was different. It didn't feel like my home anymore. But this—Baltimore?" He lifts his hand, glancing around the street. "This isn't my home either, Stella. I don't know where I'm headed, but I know this isn't my end. I won't be working the docks until I die. I won't live in this crowded city forever."

Home. I haven't thought of that word for so long. It's been years since I had one—long before Jozef and Mania, even before father's death. I've felt like a stranger in another's home ever since. We are all strangers here—at least that's what Franz used to say. I never liked that. I always hoped that there would come a time when I didn't feel that way.

"And you? Will you stay here forever, washing clothes?" Mike asks, interrupting my thoughts.

I shake my head, shrugging. "I don't know what my life will become. I'm just grateful for another day with food, another day with work, and another day with a roof over my head. I think it's more that many have."

He smiles at my response. "I suppose it is more than most, but not enough for anyone."

Not enough for anyone—the words strike me.

Mike stares down at me. "Thanks for coming to breakfast," he says, biting his lip.

"And Stella, I wanted to ask you one other thing. Are you glad I came back?"

My heart tugs at me, and I stumble for a fitting reply. I can't help but look up at Mike, and seeing his anticipation of my answer, I ask my own. "Was it worth it to you to come back?"

He exhales once more, the edges of his lips curling. There's kindness in his face, a softness in his expression when he looks at me. "Stella, you know it was. Won't you come dancing with me tomorrow night?"

I smile, my heart racing. I make it a point to meet his gaze. "I've been hoping you'd ask."

Thirty-One

Gotowe zdrowie, kto chorobie powie.
A problem shared is a problem halved.

"Stella," is all she says, tears pooling.

Valeria hasn't been herself. She's been in a daze, even burned the corner of a cotton dress earlier this morning with the iron.

I set down the parcel and wrapping, walking to her side. "Valeria, what's wrong?"

"Wrong? I'm afraid to tell you my news, for it will greatly affect you and the other girls." She wipes her eyes with a handkerchief, sighing.

I pull a chair from the desk, pushing it beside her. "Sit for a moment," I say, crouching in front of her, taking her hands in mine. "Valeria, you've been so good to me. Don't be afraid. What is it?"

Beads of sweat drip along her hairline and forehead. The bags beneath her eyes are darker, more pronounced than usual. She squeezes my hands for support. "Stella, what would you say if I told you that Mr. Gerbat wants to marry me?"

I smile. "That's wonderful news, isn't it?"

Valeria gives a faint sigh. "It is, Stella. It's just that I'm getting older, and this work is hard on me. Mr. Gerbat's job as landlord affords him free rent and much more money than Ana and I have ever seen. He could take care of us in a way that I've only dreamt about." She winces, hesitating to say more.

"But what, Valeria? This is wonderful news for you and Ana."

She looks at me again, her eyes filling with fresh tears. "As a wife, Mr. Gerbat doesn't want me working like this. He doesn't want me to keep the business."

Not keep the business? I twist my skirt, fighting off emotion. "Then you are closing down the laundering?" I ask.

Valeria nods.

I lay my head on her lap and offer weakly, "We'll be alright, the other girls and me. We'll find a way. We have so far, and we will again."

Valeria shakes her head, choked tears escaping. "I'm so sorry, Stella. It's been a hard decision, you see. I've struggled to know what to do. But this is best for Ana and me. I hope you can understand that."

I force a smile. "Of course, I do, and so will the other girls. No one can blame you for looking out for yourself and your daughter. We're grateful to you. I don't know what I would have done had I stayed in the factory. You saved me, Valeria."

Echoes of footsteps ring down the metal staircase, and Valeria and I stand, wiping at our eyes. The other girls talk and laugh, carrying their baskets of laundry.

"Not a word, Stella."

I nod, making my way back to the parcels.

The two girls set their baskets beside the ironing tables. They don't seem to notice that Valeria's eyes are red or that she irons the same dress as before they left.

I've always noticed what others don't. Even when I don't wish to, I see the details—a sullen glance, an impatient stance, an implied meaning. Perhaps I learned this unspoken language at an early age, when my mother and father died. Perhaps I learned from watching, instead of speaking.

Many think I am too serious, too quiet, but I am only waiting—waiting for the truth within the details, the words underneath the unspoken.

When the day's work is done, I sit in my room, hoping to find some peace to reconcile my future, but the girls giggle and gossip in a nearby room, making it difficult. When will Valeria tell them? Perhaps when the engagement is announced; she likes to do things in the right order, in the right way.

I don't know where I'll go.

There's always the factory. I know Mr. Pruski would hire me again. But I can't bring myself to go there again, not after being here with Valeria and Ana. The pay and conditions have been so much better. I still shiver when I think of the fire, being locked in that building like livestock or one of the sewing machines itself.

No, I can't go back.

Perhaps another laundering business? I must.

A knock at my door sounds.

"Yes?" I say, pulling myself off the bed.

"Mike is here," Valeria says through the muffled laughter of the other girls. "He says you were going to go dancing tonight?"

I rush toward the door, cracking it open. "Tell him I'm coming," I say between staggered breaths.

There's little time to straighten my dress, little time to fix my hair, and even less time to compose myself, but I determine to act my part, as if this day is no different from any other.

He stands in the front archway, wearing a newly pressed shirt. His hair is parted to the side, and he smells of pomade. I don't think I've ever seen him look so handsome, so perfect.

"You're beautiful," he says, grinning.

I try to smile. "Thanks, Mike." My eyes fall to the floor.

"Let's go," he says, shaking his head at the giggling girls behind me. He pulls my arm into his, and we walk down the broken pavement. "What's wrong?" Mike asks, touching my hand.

It always surprised me how well he guessed at my thoughts or my feelings before, and I'm glad to see he still speaks my language. He sees the details. I can't hide anything from Mike, but then again—I don't know if I want to hide anything from him now. Talking to him feels right.

"Can we sit for a moment?" I ask, stopping at a nearby bench.

Mike nods, leading me by the arm.

"Valeria is closing down her laundry business after she marries. I'll only have a job for another few weeks."

Mike's eyes soften. "And you don't know what you'll do?"

I shake my head. "I can't return to the factory; I can't go back to the way things were before, especially now that Tia is gone. I can't go back, not after the fire." My eyes burn, but I won't allow myself to cry. It's nothing compared to what I've endured. "I'll find new work. I've done it before, and I can do it again."

Mike moves closer, speaking in a hushed way, almost soft. "Stella, there's always a way out. There's plenty of work in the city. Maybe—" He stops, his lips pressing together in a line.

"Maybe what?" I ask, hopeful he really does hold an answer.

He shakes his head. "You'll find something. You always do; you're independent and strong, Stella."

I sigh, trying to make sense of everything. "I don't know, Mike. Sometimes I think there's nothing guiding me at all. I try to make my life better; I work hard and work some more, only to be thrown about by circumstance again."

Mike smiles, his eyes seeming to laugh. "That sounds about right." He throws his head back and breathes deeper. "But you keep going." He pauses once more and speaks again. "Stella, have you ever considered this fight might be better, easier even, if you weren't fighting it alone?"

Abandoned by a mother and father, mistreated by my brothers—I learned to fight alone from an early age. Does anyone have help in conquering life's battles? No one could teach Mania to be happy; no one could bring Lodzia back for Andzre; and no one could make the journey to America for me.

"I don't mean that life is easier," Mike says, as if reading my thoughts. He leans forward. "It's just easier to keep going when you have someone by your side, someone you know will support you."

He grasps my hand, lacing his fingers in mine.

My mind flashes to Oliwjer and Andzrejek and the ride on their cart, then to Marja on the train, Beata and Petar on the boat, Tia at the factory, and Valeria at the shop. I can't say these people were always at my side, but they were there for a moment, and they did make the load seem lighter, even surmountable at times.

I meet his gaze, lifting a brow. "And who should I enlist to help me?" I ask. "My brothers can't care for me; Tia is gone; Valeria is to be married. Are you volunteering?"

Mike smiles, nodding. "I asked you before if you'd marry me, and the offer still stands. Marry me, Stella. Let's leave Baltimore and start over again, together. I've already considered Pennsylvania, Chicago—even the mines out West. I'd never take your freedom, nor your independence. I only want you in my life."

I turn from his warm eyes, crossing my arms.

Life with Mike wouldn't be perfect. In fact, in some ways it would be more difficult. We're both so stubborn, so independent. We'd argue. But then again, we understand each other. I trust Mike; he's honest all of the time, even when it's painful. He tells me when I'm right and when I'm wrong. He tells me the truth even when he knows I won't agree.

If he says he wishes to marry me, he means it. He's not as self-sacrificing as Andzre, not so good to marry me only to take care of me.

"You would not want to control me, like so many men do?" My heart feels too exposed, and I worry Mike will see how badly I want to accept him.

But I must hear his answer.

"Even if I tried, we both know you wouldn't allow yourself to be subjected to such treatment," he says, smiling. The creases by his eyes soften, the curve of his lips falling. "But I could never do that, and I wouldn't want to. I care about you, Stella. I love you."

I turned Mike down once before, but it was out of fear, desperation for my independence. That choice haunted me, tugging at my heart each time he came to mind, each time I closed my eyes and saw his face. I can't bear to lose him again.

Mike stands, interrupting my thoughts. "No sense begging for an answer tonight. I think you've had a long enough day. Perhaps you should turn in for the night," he says, helping me to my feet.

I stare up at him, aware of his sudden change in mood. His wrinkled brows speak of his distress, his downcast eyes his disappointment in my silence. We walk a few paces, and I try to compose myself. I wish I had a mother to tell me how these things are done.

"Mike, I love you. I want to marry you."

He mumbles something under his breath. "What now? Rejecting me so fast?"

I push my way in front of him, forcing him to face me. "I said I love you, and I want to marry you."

Mike's mouth falls open, his eyes beaming. "You will?"

I nod.

He clears his throat, grinning. "Clairton, Pennsylvania," he says, wiping the shock from his face.

"Clairton?" I ask. I had hoped for some romantic gesture.

"They say there's more than enough work to go around. Steel mills, coal mines, barrel plants. I'm sure there's laundry services there too. There's a borough just outside of it called Braddock. There are a hundred families settled there from Croatia, some that I know. We could leave after the wedding."

"You've been thinking on this for some time then?" Warmth spreads across my chest, my cheeks hot against my hand.

He's only been waiting for me.

"How much time do you need?" he asks.

I shrug. "I suppose a couple weeks to finish my work with Valeria. And then there's the marriage license and the church. I imagine it could all be arranged quickly."

We stop at the front of the shop. I'm not sure what I expected when I accepted his offer, but something more than what he has said and done.

Mike meets my eye with understanding.

Then, for what feels like the first time in my life, I am kissed. There's strength in his arms, yet gentleness in his touch. The kiss isn't long, but it's enough to confirm that Mike isn't marrying me to take care of me. He wants me by his side. He wants me as his wife.

He loves me.

Thirty-Two

Stara miłość nie rdzewieje.
True love never grows old.

Leaving Valeria and Ana is easier than I supposed. It isn't that goodbye is easy. Valeria had, after all, taken me in at a time when I didn't think I could go on. She gave me work, a bed to sleep in, and a sense of familiarity that I hadn't felt since Beata's family on the boat. Ana had become my shadow this last year. She followed me everywhere and hung on my every word. I feel a sisterly love for her.

Yet saying goodbye isn't as grueling as I'd imagined. Maybe it's because I know that they'll be taken care of by Mr. Gerbat. Perhaps it's because I know where I am headed. Or maybe it's because I say goodbye with gratitude in my heart. I know they came into my life for a reason, but time and God have new things in store for me.

Valeria and Ana will take their place beside all those other friends in my life: Andzrejek and Oliwjer, Marja, Beata and Igor, Petar, Tia, and even Vic. Each of them helped me along my struggles, and I can only hope that I helped them in return.

Going with Mike is like writing a piece of my own life story. It comes easier than my stories to Bronia, less forced than my work at the factory, infinitely more satisfying than the sweet bread at the cafe, and for all I can hope, happier than any other journey.

The ceremony is short, only a dozen or so close friends attend. I leave the church, clinging to my old bag in one hand and Mike's arm with the other. We board an evening train following our marriage.

I sit here, too nervous to say much. There's so much ahead that's unclear.

Mike offers a small smile. "You're quiet," he says, teasing me.

I try to laugh, but it only comes out as a shaky breath. "I guess I never expected this."

His arms wrap around my waist, and he leans to look out the window. The sky is just starting to darken. He motions toward a light in the distance. "The first star of the evening. Do you think it's guiding this train?"

His words, though spoken casually, take me to another place, a place I had almost forgotten, or at least wished to forget—the ship. All at once I am standing there beside Petar again, and I remember his question.

"Do you think that is the star directing the ship?" he asked. "I do not know if they use the stars as guides any more, but they did once. Do you think there is a star guiding each of us?"

Is there something that guides me? Maybe a star, or perhaps something even greater? I stare past my reflection to the fleck in the sky. It's small, barely visible even.

I turn toward Mike, who stares down at me, a protectiveness in his expression and arms.

"I think it is," I say.

Mike pulls me in closer, and I rest my head on his shoulder.

The warmth of his cheek against my forehead reminds me that my journey is not over. Perhaps it's only beginning. Still, there's someone beside me. There's comfort along the way.

Author's Note

The stories of my great-grandmother Stella, have been passed around our family tree for some time. What is considered fact by one relative is fiction to another. Since she's no longer with us, there's no way to tell what is true and what isn't. For most of her life, Stefania Marzewska, known to us as Stella, was a very private woman. She and my great-grandfather Mike, did not speak of the "old country," until later years. After their deaths, my mother and grandmother began exchanging letters about Stella's and Mike's life and immigration journeys. It was only then that we captured much of what is written here. Though I admit most of the story is fictionalized, the premise is real. Stella's parents both died when she was young, and it is rumored she was mistreated by her brother's family in Durliosy, Poland. She came to America somewhat secretly to join a different brother in 1906. She came, like so many before and after her, for a new life, a new start. She had hope she could build something more than the life she left in Poland, and it is in this light that I wrote *The Forgotten Girl*. There are stories that she worked for a laundering service, Mike at the docks. There are also stories of a falling out between Marco and Mike surrounding Stella. One relative recalls hearing that Mike "won" Stella's hand in a game of cards against her brother.

For so many of us, the tests of poverty and tyranny are behind us, and we sometimes forget what a blessed place we live in and the people that got us here. But it's my hope that we ever remember those that came before us and what they sacrificed. Theirs is a story of resilience, hope, and freedom—a fact that should give us great comfort. Their stories are our own, their blood ours, and their character embedded within our own. Let us never forget them.

Stella's Potica Recipe

Potica (paw-tee'-tzah)

1 oz. or 2 Tbsp. yeast	3 eggs
⅔ cups lukewarm water	½ cup butter
6 cups flour	¾ Tbsp. salt
1 cup milk	1 cup sugar

Scald milk in sauce pan, add butter and melt and cool until warm.

Dissolve yeast in lukewarm water, and add 1 cup flour in yeast. Beat eggs well and add butter-milk mixture, plus salt and sugar and add to yeast. Add rest of flour and knead, brush top with melted butter and let rise until double in bulk, about 1 hour.

Filling

1 lb. ground walnuts	2 tsp. vanilla
1 cup cream (or evap. milk)	½ cup honey
2 tsp. cinnamon	1 cup sugar
3 eggs	

Mix cinnamon with walnuts. Mix cream with honey, add sugar and vanilla, and heat mixture until sugar dissolves, pour over nuts and mix well. Add beaten eggs and mix well. Now mix is ready—it should be thin enough to spread but not runny. Roll out dough thin, spread filling over dough and roll into "S" shape and place on a greased pan, and let rise 1 hour. Bake in moderate oven 350 degrees, 60–75 min. Don't overbake. Raisins may be sprinkled over filling if desired.

Discussion Questions

1. It's common for people to think "Life will be better when . . ." In what ways does Stella's life get easier, and in what ways harder, after she arrives in Fells Point?

2. Stella disapproves of boxing, believing it to be morally wrong. Is she correct in her assessment, or is Mike right in defending his profession as a means to survival? Where is the line when it comes to survival vs. morality? Is Stella right in her decision to leave Bronia in order to survive? Is Vic's gambling behavior acceptable as a method of his survival?

3. Stella is fiercely independent because of the hardships she has had to endure. How do her friends on the ship teach her the importance of companionship? How do her friends in Fells Point teach her this same thing?

4. Stella realizes she cares about Mike after he has already returned to Croatia. Why was she so wary of him before his departure?

5. In what ways did each character help or hinder Stella's journey to America, and eventually to happiness? How did Stella help others along their own journeys? Does anybody ever live a life independent of others, or are we all interconnected like the characters in the story?

6. Stella left Poland to find freedom. Did she ever find it? And if so, was it different than what she thought it would be?

7. What sacrifices did Stella, and so many immigrants like her, make in coming to America in the early 1900s?

Acknowledgments

"At times our own light goes out and is rekindled by a spark from another person. Each of us has cause to think with deep gratitude of those who have lighted the flame within us."
—Albert Schweitzer

A story is much like a puzzle—pieces from different times, places, and people coming together to form a picture. I'm grateful for those that have 'lit the flame within me' and provided a missing piece to this story. To all those that helped, thank you. To my sisters, Melissa and Becky: You have been my champions, cheering me on at my lowest points. You read draft after draft, brainstormed with me during late-night telephone conversations, and came to love these characters almost as much as I do. To my husband, Mark: You've been the greatest support I could hope for. I love how you want me to succeed, how you believe I can do anything I set my mind to. To my great-grandmother Stella: You've inspired me in a huge way, and I hope this story carries your strength to others. To my Heavenly Father: Thank you for giving me words, and for allowing me to share them with others. To Cedar Fort: Thank you for taking another chance on me and providing the help I needed—Hali Bird and Jessica Romrell as editors, Vikki Downs at marketing, and Priscilla Chaves and Katie Payne in designing the loveliest cover I could have hoped for. And lastly, to my readers: Thank you for listening.

About the Author

Being the youngest of four sisters and one very tolerant older brother, Heather grew up on a steady diet of chocolate, *Anne of Green Gables*, Audrey Hepburn, Jane Austen, and the other staples of female literature and moviedom. These stories, along with good teachers, encouraged Heather throughout high school and college to read many of the classics in literature, and later, to begin writing her own stories of romance and adventure. After meeting and marrying her husband, Mark, Heather graduated magna cum laude from Brigham Young University and finally settled down in a small farming community in southeastern Idaho with her husband and four children. In her spare time, Heather enjoys time spent with family, volleyball, piano, the outdoors, and almost anything creative.

Scan to Visit

www.heatherchapmanauthor.com